For Love's Sake

For Love's Sake

Michelle McGriff

Writers Club Press
San Jose New York Lincoln Shanghai

For Love's Sake

Writers Club Press
an imprint of iUniverse.com, Inc.

For information address:
iUniverse.com, Inc.
5220 S 16th, Ste. 200
Lincoln, NE 68512
www.iuniverse.com

This is a work of fiction. All people, places, and incidents that reseamble actual people and places and incidents, are purely coincidental.

ISBN: 0-595-15105-1

DEDICATION

To my mother who always said: "Before you leave a room...look back...make sure you picked up all your stuff."

To my son Jordan, I love you...even with blue hair.

To my baby daughter Qiara, sorry, but you really aren't going to get any taller.

To my eldest Danielle, thank you for never letting me miss a day of reality.

And to Thomas...don't say me Monkey.

ACKNOWLEDGEMENTS

I would like to thank my reading group; you are always there to help me when I need encouragement or advice. A special thanks to Wanda for proofreading this for me, your help was invaluable. Joanne thanks for your help and friendship. I promise you will one-day 'get' fiction…just let your mind go with it…just give into the lack of logic and you're there. But in the meantime, I appreciate your ability to rein me in from time to time. Your knowledge of the law seems to come so easy, and you had an answer for everything. You will be a great lawyer. Just remember that I knew you when…and I have pictures to prove it! To my professors at Ventura College, thanks again for your support, especially Deborah Ventura…*the nuns would be proud*. To Barbara Jean for helping me develop the characters of this story and Heather for your feedback and making me feel special. Heather, you are a talented lady, don't give into the weight of reality…it's only as heavy as you let it be. Yolanda and Jenna, for always making me laugh. To my sister and mother for being proud of me. I believe that you are proud of me, but I still need to hear it and you've both been really good about that. Aunt Ella I am so glad that you really like what I write and not just because I wrote it. Gary I've decided that your job in life is simply to remind me how deep love really goes, how much it hurts, how long it really last and how impossible it is to recover from.

INTRODUCTION

In the world of tightly wrapped professionals, some might say, letting one's hair down in public, using slang, improper grammar or being politically incorrect is 'unacceptable'. Crossing the economic lines, fraternizing with those in lower social arenas 'inexcusable', and trusting someone else, based on a gut instinct…without a contract, just down-right 'unrealistic'. These were Nigel's thoughts, anyway…before his life was changed by a dream; a recurring dream directing him to follow his heart…something all too new and frightening for him to even contemplate.

PROLOGUE

The fog rolled in as he approached the Golden Gate Bridge. Its massive, orange metal legs stretched high into the clouds beyond his view. The foghorn could be heard now, right on cue. Resisting the urge to look over the railing was impossible. Once again today, the Captain would wave in that all-too-familiar way. And the people, all dancing, drinking; he could hear them laughing. And then the music would start…What was the name of that song? It didn't matter. She would be here soon; he could feel it. There were people on the lookout, and they were calling to the people on the boat, and then the people on the boat would call to him. Even from miles away, down there in the water, he could hear them. But he couldn't hear the people on the lookout, who seemed further away though they were actually closer. The people on the boat would call out "Meet us when we dock!" But he knew he would be unable to because of an appointment he had. As he turned around, there she was, standing on the lookout. He never knew where she came from, but it didn't matter. She was so beautiful with the breeze blowing through her soft, white flowing dress. Her eyes so dark and alluring, her skin, so brown and smooth…he couldn't wait to touch her. He hoped that this time he would get to touch her…to even hold her hand. Sometimes he wouldn't get the chance. Sometimes he would wake up…

CHAPTER I

The day had gone well, at least from where Nigel stood. They had won the case, and Mrs. Lambuson was going to take it all; including the brass ring and kitchen sink. Nigel could have sworn he saw Max, her now ex-husband, literally sway back and forth as if hit with a paddle on the back of the neck, with each court order to pay something slapped on him by Judge D. Marcum.

Superior Court Judge Marcum was not known for his generosity, so Nigel knew it had to have been because of the case he had presented. He had proved, indisputably, that Mrs. Lambuson had needed a lot of money, the car, the house, the jewelry and well…a plethora of various sundries.

Under his European-cut, burnt sienna suit, Nigel had worn his lucky drawers. Those lucky underwear were the same ones that he had planned on wearing to carry him through the winning touch down of the Superbowl this weekend. He was planning on a big win then too, only at the Superbowl he would be screaming a lot louder, perhaps even making a few animal noises. But not today, today he would have to stay cool and collected.

Even now, behind his cool facial expression, he wanted to pull his fist back in a mannerism of victory and yell out 'Yessss'…as he had won yet another big one and had gotten everything asked for by his client.

It wasn't so much that he felt the now ex-Mrs. Lambuson was so upright, true and deserving; it was more the fact that the Mr. was loaded, and Nigel had just nailed a bundle for the firm!

This case had been going on for almost a year, and now, it would be over. They would all party…he and his associates. They would drink, tell lies, and have a ball. The day was good.

He had gotten so deep into the mood of the upcoming evening that he had almost missed the date of the custody hearing for his client's two children. 'Poor slob,' he thought of Mr. Lambuson. Here he was about to hand over more than a customary amount of his assets, and still he wanted more than just an occasional weekend with his children. 'What a glutton for punishment,' Nigel thought and with that, he fought back a chuckle by coughing.

He really didn't know why he found the thought of the man wanting to see his children remotely amusing, but he had to reason that perhaps it was the whole concept of fatherhood that bewildered him. He never completely understood the strange power these little people (children, or better yet, babies) had on adults. But he did understand this; it was one thing to make a baby, but quite another to be a father, and that difference was not one that he had any intention of discovering.

"Problem, Mr. Godwins?" Judge Marcum sneered. Nigel shook his head. He knew the judge didn't like him. Not too many of the judges in this circuit did. He didn't take it personally; it was no doubt the firm he was with. Madison and Associates were known for being on the edge…the verge. They went out on legal limbs for their clients. They took on the underdogs and won for them, and they usually won a lot. They made sure they won more money than those other big guys ever dreamed of. They took on cases of any kind that had greenbacks up for grabs. Cases no one wanted to touch…criminal, domestic, and corporate. Someone in that office could handle it. If there was a Regular Joe out there who needed legal representation against the big, bad guys…Madison and Associates were there.

Nigel's specialty was domestic cases…making sure prenuptial contracts were made and kept, and if not, finding brilliant ways to get around them. Any woman, who wanted to be supported and never work again, got her wish…no matter how many affairs she had. If she didn't want her kids, she didn't get them. If she did, she got them exclusively. Every man not wanting to 'give-that-bitch-a-damn-dime' had too.

The only problem that Nigel felt was that this whole business was making him grow cold in his viewpoint of life and love. Everything was a business deal to him. If it didn't have a contract attached, how much was it really worth investing in? He knew this view of things was off base, just a little, but it was becoming a part of his thoughts. It was becoming who he was and he couldn't fight it. Even in his personal relationship with Sherry, there had been no contract and so no real commitment, though he would never have admitted that to anyone.

Nigel knew, deep inside, he was turning into a cold, middle-aged man and soon it would start showing. Sometimes, his associate and personal friend, Terrell McAllister would let him know that time was ever approaching…like now.

"You don't care about anybody, Nyge. You don't…and before you open your mouth to say you do…you don't." Terrell began his usual, playful harassment that always came after Nigel would finish describing his legal agility and prowess used in winning a case.

Terrell's large smile and pearly white teeth flashing gave his face an almost innocent appearance. Though his appearance said one thing, as the firm's corporate lawyer, Nigel knew him to be one of the most aggressive and tenacious people he had ever met. Nigel was often glad he would never have to find himself pitted against him in a courtroom.

Terrell was about five eight in bare feet, but with the gym-created-bulk that he carried on his frame, he looked bigger.

He was single…well, as single as Nigel was. He had Rita and Nigel had Sherry.

Terrell and Rita, a psychologist who worked for the high school counseling department, seemed well-suited for each other, though evenings out with them as a couple would tire Sherry out completely. Perhaps it was the love they had for their ethnicity, or how both could so easily slide from their expensive business suits and corporate attitudes into loud, playful and sometimes argumentative banter filled with Ebonics.

This use of the language seemed almost second nature to Nigel, coming from his third generation Sicilian background and having a Grandfather who sometimes seemed to speak a similar language, as he would on occasion speak English in his own invented way…a little Italian…a little English.

He was one of Nigel's favorite people.

The evening with the four of them together, would go completely over Sherry's head-Terrell and Rita using their choice of casual language, and Nigel also using it freely, much to Sherry's dismay.

Nigel would watch her frustration grow out of the corner of his eye. He would sometimes even enjoy watching her lack of understanding. She was always so in-the-know about everything and everyone…all the time. It was to the point of being irritating and haughty. Perhaps it was just his pride, but he felt, serious competition on *every* issue just didn't seem necessary, and seeing her humbled from time to time was what he enjoyed.

He knew he shouldn't feel this way. Sherry was someone he claimed to have deep feelings for. But he knew there had always been something very wrong in their relationship, in his opinion. He just had never completely been able to put his finger on it.

Sherry was what Nigel called '*white-bred*'. It wasn't her fault, and he tried to appreciate that.

She came from old money, cultured pearls and pedigree cats. Her father was CEO of Cruxtonoden, a construction company that he had built with his own hands. He, having formally worked for his own father, now laid claims that his company would revolutionize the pre-fabricated home. So far, it hadn't; but stocks in the company were soar-ing and he was getting richer by the day.

However, coming from one of Utah's more wealthier families, even if he had decided one day to just stop working, no one in his family line would ever have to worry from one day to the next where they would eat or sleep; which was very different from Nigel's background. He could often think back to days when there was not too much more than what was *needed*…and almost not that much.

Sherry worked for Daddy in his company. She had since she was eighteen. Smart and aggressive, Daddy knew he had something good in this kid. When she was thirteen she wanted to buy stocks and get into the market. She was a no-nonsense player when it came to making money.

She pictured herself to be tops in her field and perhaps it was true. There hadn't been too many good deals that had gotten away from her, which often made her wonder about her relationship with Nigel. She was a great salesperson, but not good enough to sell Nigel on the idea that marriage and a family would be right for them…it wasn't for lack of trying. Often she had to step back and wonder if she was slip-ping…or perhaps Nigel wasn't all that great of a deal.

Sherry had been willing to live with him for almost three years now without the consent on his part to marry or give her any children. She was not quite thirty and wanted a family. Her biological clock was tick-ing, in her opinion. Besides, she was the only one of her six siblings that hadn't produced an heir to her father's legacy.

Nigel never understood why she stayed with him either, and he would admit that freely. He was always saying and doing the wrong things, he hated her friends and most of her family.

He wondered deep inside, how much longer this relationship could last.

"Let's get married," Sherry said, with all the depth of an impulse, one morning before they left to go off in their different directions.

"Then we would need a prenuptial," Nigel remarked, without hesitation. He then grinned slyly as he gulped down his orange juice. It was a joke, and he was hoping his meaning had come out right. Sherry's cold stare showed him it hadn't.

"Listen honey," he began an attempt to repair the developing situation as Sherry grabbed her tapestry-covered briefcase off the dinette chair and stormed out of the condo, swinging the front door back and nearly hitting him in the face.

"Sherry, honey, look I didn't mean it the way it came out," he pleaded for forgiveness as they reached their parking stalls. Sherry enjoyed exchanging her convertible Mercedes each year for a new color. This year the color was red.

"Forget about it," she said in that overly perky way that meant, very clearly to him, that there was no way she would ever forget about it. She smiled tightly and flipped back her blonde hair as she climbed into her convertible.

"Come on baybee don't do me like dat," Nigel began to flirt. He leaned in the window to kiss her goodbye, but she pulled back just enough for him to miss the mark. She pulled her sunglasses down from the visor and put them on.

The weatherman had predicted no rain today, so there was no threat from the normal, coastal overcast. This meant to Sherry that the ragtop would come down, and she would clear her head as the wind blew through her hair on the way to the office.

"Don't call me baby like that; you sound like Terrell," she grimaced.

"You didn't seem to mind it last night." His words were cool and showed his immediate dislike for the implication in her comment. Her smile softened slightly as she touched his face.

"Let's not fight. Call Terrell and Rita and let's go out with them tonight or something," she spoke on in her insincerity. Nigel knew he wouldn't ask Terrell to go out tonight, not under an offer like that one.

That was over six months ago, and they hadn't talked directly about marriage again, though the indirect resentment had weighed heavy over their relationship since that morning.

Today, Terrell was working on a takeover of one of the local Internet Service Providers (ISP) by a larger one. It was an easy maneuver on his part, as he was on the side of the larger one...

"*The Eater*", as he called them.

"I thought you were suppose to be in front of Judge Montgomery, the Albino," Terrell asked, straightening out his papers. Although he loved making indirect racial slurs when he could get away with it, in the case of Judge Montgomery, there was no racism even remotely intended. The man was fairer than any other white man either of them had ever seen before. Though they knew he was not a true albino by genetics, he had to have been close.

"Bailed again. He recused himself. I don't know what's up with that."

"What personal issue does he have with you?" Terrell asked.

"I don't know, but it keeps happening. Getting a chance to be in his courtroom is almost becoming an obsession for me. I want to get a shot at him, if for no other reason than because I hear rumor that he never does that until I'm suppose to appear in front of him...next thing you know, I get some other guy like Judge Marcum, who hates my guts. I'm surprised I won. I think Montgomery hates my guts too. Why else would he go through the trouble to recuse? I'd like to get a chance to tangle with that ol' Albino man," Nigel jeered as he pretended to grapple with the chair.

"You know, I hear the man is a true albino. You could get a spell put on you or something if he really does hate you. He could turn your hair as white as his. They have special powers. My granny told me about them. I'd be glad I never got him if I were you. Never look deep into those white eyes of his," Terrell's voice took on a sinister tone as he crouched low, imitating a wild animal of some kind stalking his prey, ready to pounce.

"I've only seen him from a distance. He stared at me and then took off in the other direction. Scared the sh…" Nigel began.

Just then the senior partner, Dave Madison, entered the conference room where Nigel and Terrell were hiding out, talking over the day. Dave had a client with him. She looked familiar, but neither Terrell nor Nigel could place her under that large hat that hid a good portion of her face. And they both knew that, no matter how long they stared at her long, shapely, freshly-waxed legs that wasn't going to help them know her any better either. Dave cleared his throat as Nigel quickly released the chair.

"Sorry fellas didn't know you were in here. Perhaps you can allow me some time with the conference room here to consult with a perspective, new client," Dave said using his fatherly voice that meant business first, playtime later.

Dave was a push over by nature. Nigel knew that from having had drinks with the man. He had gotten to see first hand how easily Dave could be made to laugh and pay for rounds of cognac…the best kind.

He had inherited the hot seat as senior partner from his father, old man Madison, when he retired. Now, he was bound by blood to keep the firm in tact and not let its reputation slip an ounce. So far, in the fifteen years he had held the first seat, he hadn't.

Even before Nigel had started there, some seven or so years ago as a kid fresh out of law school, he had heard of the reputation of Madison and Associates. They had never lost a case. Not one worth remembering anyway. They advertised on TV and on the billboards that he would see as he sat stuck in traffic on the freeway heading to South San Francisco, where he was born and raised. Nigel had been so impressed with them, even then, and he could hardly believe it when he had actually been invited to join their firm. *Invited*!

He remembered the day.

He had just gotten home from his position at the District Attorney's office. He worked in the Family Support Division in downtown Richmond. It had been his first real job since graduation.

He had done his apprenticeship there. Liking his work and the way he handled himself with clients, they offered him a job immediately after he graduated.

"You got a call today. It was a job offer, I think," his mother said casually as she tossed a green salad.

She always had a big dinner waiting as if they were a large family instead of just the two of them. No matter how tight things got, cooking was never shorted.

It had always been the two of them, as Nigel's father had been killed on the way to the hospital the night of his birth.

It was a tragic story really and each time it was told it seemed to grow in drama and detail until now it would almost make her cry even before she would start to tell it. It had gotten so bad that by his teens Nigel usually stayed far from any kind of father type conversation with her as he could. She was such an emotional woman.

"Job offer…you think?" he asked in the same casual manner as she. He skimmed through the mail that sat on a small entry table by the door. There was a pregnant pause as she wiped her hands on her apron before coming into the corridor where he was.

He always remembered that day because; she never looked him directly in the eye as she spoke. He had learned from his grandfather; this mannerism was usually a sign of a lie being told. But Nigel listened…it was his mother after all. She never lied to him before, so he just knew this couldn't be one of those times.

"I like the way you handled that chair," Ms…Dave's client said. Her voice was deep and sultry. Nigel felt his face grow warm as he straightened his tie and smoothed back his sandy blonde hair. "and, nice tan too," she continued her flirtation, noticing his Mediterranean complexion. She had to wonder which salon he went too. His tan was perfect, not too light not too dark and no streaks…

"Thanks, but it's not a tan," he corrected quickly. "I was just demonstrating to Terrell how we handle the opposition here at Madison and Associates," Nigel ad-libbed, to explain the man handling of the chair. Terrell cleared his throat and nodded.

"I got it but I think you should show me one more time so I can be sure," he joked, imitating a headlock with an invisible victim.

"I'll show you outside," Nigel said quickly and the two of them started for the door.

"Oh fellas, before you go I'd like to introduce you to Mrs. Winston Montgomery," Dave said slowly and spoke more with his eyes than his words. Nigel felt his mouth drop open and he saw Terrell's do the same.

"We will be representing her in her," he paused. "da-vorce," he continued slowly, almost spelling the word divorce.

"From Judge Montgomery?" Nigel asked before he could stop himself. "The albi…"

Terrell grabbed his arm tight.

"Uh, Nyge means, uh…never mine what he means. We will talk with you later, Dave." He then rescued the situation by dragging stiffened and mortified Nigel into the hall.

"Are you nuts? Calling that overly white man an albino in front of his, over sexed and no doubt adulteress wife? Are you nuts? We are about to take the case of Judge Montgomery's divorce. And we are on the 'her' side. Oh my Gawd; and she liked your tan, man." Terrell put his hands up to his mouth in mock shock and then gave him a high five.

Lydia, the legal secretary saw the two of them all but jumping up and down, dancing with each other in the hallway, she smirked at their unprofessional behavior.

"Oh stop it girl, you know what that means her being in there. And you just about fainted when she walked in," Terrell harassed her as they walked over to the counter surrounding her desk.

"No I don't know what that means, and don't call me girl and I won't call you boy," she said giving Terrell the reality check he needed.

The two of them were the only African Americans in the office. Often Terrell wanted that to mean an instant bond of understanding between them however, Lydia was Lydia and he was Terrell, and soon he had to realize that the color of their skin was all they had in common and ever would.

Lydia was strict and ultra-professional. She had been working in that law office since long before he had come on the scene.

She had filed and kept that office in running order for old man Madison during the Civil Rights movement, when he represented many blacks and won many unpopular cases. She even had a large picture of Rosa Parks on her wall, personally autographed by the woman herself, *or so she said.*

Lydia was a legend and not to be played with.

She knew her way around a law office and had seen many young upstarts come and go.

Though old man Madison seemed to have a lot of respect for African Americans, none of them had been a part of that firm until Terrell.

It was because of her; Terrell had been brought on board.

She had made acquaintance with Terrell's father and mother during their college days. They had continued their friendship long after graduating, keeping in touch often.

Garret, Terrell's father, taught at the University of San Francisco as a political science professor before his death from cancer. He had made large steps to keep his family out of the grips of poverty. So even after his death, Lucille, his wife, was able to provide for herself and Terrell well enough. But when she too died unexpectedly, and Terrell was sent to live with Lucille's parents, Lydia knew Garret and Lucille McAllister wanted more for their child than to end up lost in a world of archaic thinking, only to emerge, neck deep in mediocrity.

Being unmarried and childless and with no desire to change either status, Lydia took on Terrell as a project. She became a secret benefactor to him, making sure he continued his education and never had to leave law school.

She was so proud of him when he graduated five years ago. She immediately used her history with old man Madison to get Terrell added to the firm under his son Dave. Lydia never wanted Terrell to know anything about the part she played in his life and to this day he didn't. He was a proud young man, just like she remembered his father Garret being. Terrell figured it was only through his hard work and pure luck he had made it to where he was. It seemed to make him work harder viewing his accomplishments this way. Lydia drew a quiet sense of pride deep inside with each achievement he made. She knew he would never make full partner but who could say...maybe one day he and his crazy friend Nigel might strike out on their own. They were both certainly talented enough to succeed.

"Why do you hate me so, Lydia?" Terrell asked, his voice full of imitated penance.

"I don't hate you, Terrell. I just don't like the way you act sometimes...most of the time," she said, flashing him a warm forgiving smile. "And if you were my boy, I'd have to beat you," she added.

"I knew you loved me." He winked. Suddenly he snapped his finger in the air as a thought flashed into his head. "Oh and I did my part for humanity. Put down that I gave blood the other day; lot's of it. Put down, 'Terrell gave lot's of blood,'" he said, leaning over the counter of her reception area in his attempt to read her daily planning calendar.

This calendar was where she simply kept appointments, but guarded as if it contained secret reports on everyone's coming and goings. She acted as if it did the way she shielded it whenever anyone would get close to it. Even now, she covered its pages as Terrell leaned in close.

"Took you long enough," she said, rolling her eyes at Terrell and then looking to Nigel for a comment on what he had done for humanity.

"And you Mr. Godwins? And don't give me that 'I'm afraid of needles' stuff or that other one. What did Peterson say? Oh yeah, 'I don't have a heart so how can I make blood'…now you know that's some crap."

"I donated," Nigel, said under his breath as he noticed a spot on his shoe and bent over to wipe it off.

It was true, what his grandpa had said. People really never made eye contact when lying, even if when sort of lying. Here he was down here cleaning his shoe while telling Lydia a half-truth.

Once again Nigel realized how amazing his grandfather was.

Nigel had made a donation all right but it wasn't to the blood bank and there was no way he was telling her that he had donated to the sperm bank downtown.

Dave had just said to donate to a life giving resource-or something like that. He was tired of lawyers getting such a bad rap.

"Nobody likes us. I mean we've been called 'heartless bloodsuckers'."

Dave was thinking out loud one Monday morning. It had been about three months ago now. They all sat around the boardroom before going over their cases. No one knew where that statement had come from but apparently Dave was feeling strongly about it. So he came up with the idea for everyone to make some kind of social statement by donating something useful to someone else. 'A gift of life', he called it 'do it for humanity', he added. Nigel was thinking perhaps Dave had seen a billboard off the freeway or a sign on a bus stop and he was just feeling noble.

Could anyone ever really know how anything that came out of Dave's mouth ever got into that brain of his? But Lydia took the minutes so she could *pester*…uh, remind everyone of his or her pledge to donate something, and it was a done deal.

"I donated clothes," Marcia Shoeman whispered under her breath the next Monday morning, as Dave reminded everyone about the pledge they had all agreed to the week before. "That very same day, I emptied my extra closet of junk and took it right down to Goodwill. I'm saving some poor badly dressed housewife from a life of poor fashion sense," she said and then smiled slyly.

"I don't think that's what he had in mind, Marcia," Nigel whispered back; Dave caught him.

"And Nigel, I know you have done your part. I won't embarrass you by asking you to tell us all what you did. I will just take note that you did something very giving and kind." Dave's tone was heavy with sarcasm.

"Yes, I have…uh…will." Nigel cleared his throat.

That very afternoon as he sat in his car in front of that blood bank with his sleeve rolled up searching madly for visible veins he knew he was sunk. It was bad enough getting that occasional vial filled during his yearly physical. He was sure the blood bank would want pints, maybe gallons! He would have to drink juice afterward and maybe even go home and rest…recover even.

Before he knew where he was or became fully cognizant of what he was doing, the pornographic magazine was in front of him and he was being driven to ejaculation at his own hand or *with* his own hand, one could say.

The dark haired woman with the nameplate that identified her simply as Mary had a friendly and surprisingly warm smile under the circumstances, he thought to himself. He had always imagined these places having beastly women who would man handle you if you were having difficulty obtaining the desired results. But this Mary was quite attractive and he felt flushed and embarrassed the next time he saw her knowing that he had been able to use her quite effectively as a mental visual and easily achieved the desired outcome. She took the specimen for testing along with only six tubes of blood. That wasn't nearly as bad as what he had envisioned the bloodletting procedure to be…and nowhere as bad as he had imagined the blood bank.

That night over dinner at their usual Monday night restaurant Sherry asked him how his day had gone. It was a simple question; one she asked everyday actually, but tonight he must have blushed because of the strange look that covered her face as he stammered, trying fill the hours of his day with contrivances instead of the facts…for the next three Mondays as he finished the donation process, the story of his day would be identical, but she never seemed to notice.

That was three months ago now and Nigel hadn't thought much about it, until today…and he certainly hadn't told anyone.

"So what was with the thing back in there with Lydia?" Terrell asked later as he had noticed Nigel's lack of eye contact with Lydia when she brought up his donation.

"Oh nothing, I just didn't want to tell her what I did."

"What did you do?" Terrell slowed his pace as they walked out to their cars.

"I…I donated sperm," Nigel said trying to sound nonchalant.

"You what?" Now Terrell stopped dead in his tracks and set his brief-case down.

"Oh, stop the drama. I donated sperm. Don't tell me you never thought about doing that."

"No, as fine as I am, I have never thought about doing that. When I get the urge to donate sperm, it goes into Rita. Are you nuts? In this day and age of super technology you act like that was an anonymous thing you did. Like nobody can hunt you down for child support somewhere down the line. Like nobody is going to be pissed at how ugly their kid is."

"Nobody is gonna hunt me down. I'm a lawyer for goodness sake, nobody is gonna hunt me down. And I'm not ugly."

"You act like…like you wanted to be a father or something. What about Sherry, she was cool with this? I know Rita would not be cool with this."

"I sorta didn't tell Sherry," Nigel admitted, feeling remorse suddenly coming on fast.

"You sorta didn't tell Sherry? Oh my Gawd, you lied to Sherry!" Terrell began looking around as he rubbed his forehead.

"I didn't lie to Sherry," Nigel defended. "I omitted."

He couldn't tell if Terrell were joking or truly upset as he covered his mouth with his hand and stood with his other hand on his hip in sudden deep thought. Finally, looking deep into Nigel's hazel eyes, he said with all seriousness, "You gotta get em back."

"Get em back? You can't just go get em back. It's been almost three months."

"Sure you can. You had to fill out some kind of identification thing, so just go down there and tell them you want them back. Tell them you need them for something. You told them you were just storing them, right? So technically they belong to you. You did tell them they were for storage, right? They weren't suppose to like, give em out or anything, right?" Terrell asked in a pleading tone. Nigel stood stiff as stone and didn't answer.

The two men dropped their heads suddenly…as if to pray.

CHAPTER 2

Qiana sat reading the latest issue of *Baby Joy* magazine while she waited for her second counseling appointment. She was prepared for whatever question they could throw at her for why she wanted a baby this way. She thought she had been clear enough on her first visit over a month ago. She was willing to pay for the procedure that day but they wouldn't let her, but again today she had brought her money.

Her insurance wasn't going to cover any of it, as she was neither infertile nor married so it was going to take a good chunk of her savings to do this. But she was ready.

'*Artificial insemination*', what a name for making a baby. Just the word 'Artificial' made it all seem so unreal. But it wasn't. This would be a child, a real living breathing life. And it would be hers, to love and raise and teach. She felt her head nod as once again her strong conviction came through.

She had done a lot of research on the procedure, and according to what she read; it wasn't going to be an awfully painful thing. She wouldn't even need to take time off work. If all went well, she would be pregnant before her birthday mid March. It would be like a present to herself. At her birthday dinner she would announce it to her family that she was pregnant. They would all suspect Rufus and she would somehow convince them of another lover, a secret lover—*no, she would simply tell the truth.*

She was almost thirty-five years old and with her biological clock ticking away, she found that she no longer had the desire to put up with Rufus and his thoughts on how her life should go. He had been a waste of three vital years of her life.

Sure she could just meet another man, but what would be point. That would take time too. And besides, she knew deep inside that she would just be using any man for his sperm, at this point. If she was going to go about finding a man with such a clinically motivated attitude, then it made more sense for her to simply cut out the middleman, as it were, and go straight to a sperm bank.

She hadn't told anyone except her best friend Rashawn and of course her friend Lorraine who worked at the *Family Makers Sperm Bank*, downtown. She was the one who had first brought up the prospects of artificial insemination to her.

"It's a newly opened sperm bank downtown. It branched off from one of the bigger ones out of San Francisco. It's the way the future my friend," Lorraine said over lunch at the Cabbage Bin, a new salad bar that had just gone up near the hospital.

Qiana gazed out the window longingly, as she watch a woman pushing her baby in a stroller.

"You just say it like that," she sighed.

"No really, when I left the hospital and started working there, I just thought it was a better paying job. I didn't really think that much about it. I mean, I've got six kids. Why would I think about artificial insemination? I mean, I may have thought about Doug doing some donating," Lorraine chuckled. "But anyway, now that I work there and I see the men who come, pardon the pun," Lorraine chuckled again. "I mean, professional men, smart, handsome men. I figured what could be the harm in taking out some of the guesswork. Don't get me wrong, I think my kids are beautiful, but if I could have *chosen*…oh my Gawd. I might have gotten some sperm that was more musically inclined or quiet-natured," she continued. "Or maybe even black," she nodded hoping to whet Qiana's appetite for the possibilities. Qiana rolled her eyes at her Caucasian friend with the heaviest Oklahoma drawl she had ever heard.

"You, with a black child? I don't think so."

"No, it coulda happened," Lorraine said sounding all together serious as she filled her mouth with croutons.

From what Qiana read from the pamphlet that Lorraine had given her, Artificial Insemination was in fact actually said to be the new way of free choice for family building in the future...sort of how the Internet had become the household word for communication.

And Lorraine did say that many professional, bright and intelligent men were donating sperm these days. Besides what could go wrong? It wasn't like when giving blood had its initial boom and so much contamination got through. There would be stringent testing and sorting and filing and..."Mistakes are rarely...if ever made," Lorraine added, sounding much like a commercial, as she tried to add confirmation to her statement.

Qiana now smiled to herself as she sat in the lobby of the *Family Makers Sperm Bank*, remembering the conversation.

She took a confident cleansing breath and once again assured herself she was doing the right thing.

"Ms. Patterson," the nurse called. Qiana jumped slightly, giggling in her embarrassment, and quickly put the magazine aside.

"It's ok to be nervous," the nurse assured, as she led her down the long hallway.

"I'm a nurse," Qiana answered, without being asked.

"Yes, that is what you told us on your paperwork, a pediatric nurse for Doctor Stewart. That's great. Your baby will have a good solid home with someone who knows what they are doing." The facilitating nurse smiled.

"Go ahead and get undressed and put on one of those gowns so we get your vitals and measure some mucus," she said, as if this were an everyday routine. But then, Qiana thought to herself, it was...for this nurse. But for Qiana, she was caught off guard, not having expected the testing to be done today. She was all ready to defend her reasons again for wanting a baby. It was suddenly as if they didn't care anymore. She had told them once and they must have believed her.

"I thought this was going to be more complicated," she said.

"Oh no, here at the *Family Makers* we figure the client knows what they want when they come here. I mean, you do know what you want, right?"

"I want a baby."

"Good, we've got plenty of those. At least the, baby making, part," she giggled slightly. "Lorraine told me that you were a friend of hers. You and Lorraine are friends, right?"

"Yes, I guess I just didn't figure that she could actually get me in this soon." Qiana started to unbutton her blouse.

"Well, looking over your chart, there's nothing to hold you up. I will be the one doing the procedure. My name is Yvonne."

"But you're a nurse."

"Well, a nurse practitioner actually. It's really not that complicated a procedure, you'll see. You'll just feel a little prick," she said and then stood, giggling…engulfed in her own private joke.

The friendly nurse practitioner smiled and walked out as Qiana finished changing into the paper robe.

This was too easy…almost disconcertingly so, she thought.

She now thought back to the day that she had made the decision to do this. It was Christmas day. She remembered it like it was yesterday. Rufus had stood her up again and she sat alone in her apartment. She had survived the embarrassment of being at her parents without her so-called boyfriend, again. Her sister, Chalice, was there with hers and her brother Charles was there with his wife and child, a beautiful little boy name Jared. His wife, Selena, kept his hair braided in two braids that nearly reached his shoulders. He was already four and looked like a little girl with his long eyelashes and all that hair. Qiana was crazy about him.

Everyone was complete but her and she had enough of that scenario.

She could tell her mother wanted to have one of those deep talks about things that were going on in her life and head but Qiana had no desire for that lecture. It came every year about this time.

"What are you going to do with your life, Qiana? When are you going to get rid of Rufus, Qiana? Why can't you be happy just nursing, Qiana? Why in God's name would you want a baby, Qiana?"

Her mother just didn't understand being a nurse was great, there was no discussion there, but not having a child was truly eating away at her; it had been for a long time. Besides, she didn't know what she was going to do about Rufus.

Rufus' real name was Russell Thompson, before his love for Reggae music and donning of dreadlocks, earned him his new name; Rufus Myduful, just about a year ago.

He had filled her life for about three years now. He was a lot of fun in the beginning but his playful, childish ways were tiring her. He wasn't serious about anything that didn't start with 'ya mon'.

He had developed an awful temper over the last couple of years too. She attributed that to his increased usage of recreational drugs.

Rufus never wanted to go around her friends or take her to dinner in nice places. He barely wanted her to go. It was just becoming the same old life with him and that life did not include family responsibilities. If it didn't involve her sitting in some smoky hemp filled underground tavern, listening to his offbeat poetry readings or hearing his band play, he was not into it.

Somehow he would always bring any type of conversation about responsibilities back around to the white man and his 'dominance over everything and everyone'.

The negative changes in their relationship were more than clear but still it continued and Qiana soon saw no way out. Rufus had indeed become very tiring.

That night after the Christmas dinner, Qiana had picked up the phone and called her girlfriend, Rashawn. She thought perhaps they could take in a movie or something, but as usual, Rashawn had a house full…a party. She was always having parties.

She was single and unattached. She lived with her sister Rita, most of the time. Well, actually it was the house they had both inherited from their grandmother. For the last few years Rita lived there only off and on. She lived the off time with her boyfriend.

Today was an on time and they were having some of her sister's boyfriend's friends over for drinks.

"Come on over anyway," Rashawn suggested. "It's just Rita and Terrell and their yuppie friends. I'm sure there will be someone here you like, someone to understand your issues. I mean, they *are* lawyers and some of them are single," she said as her voice trailed from the phone. Qiana imagined her targeting one of those single lawyers as she spoke.

"No," Qiana sighed. "I'm kinda on a downer and I wanted to bring you down with me. But it wouldn't be fair, you being at a party and all."

"What? Oh yeah, sure. Ok, so I'll see you in a bit? Ok bye," Rashawn said and hung up. Qiana chuckled to herself at her friend's lack of concern over her desperate situation.

Rashawn was a good friend, despite the ease in which she could be distracted, and the next day; she was right at the door to talk over Qiana's troubles. By the following Monday, when Qiana went back to work, she had made up her mind.

Discussing it with the doctor she worked for, Marten Stewart, he suggested she pursue it.

"I think it's a wonderful idea, Qiana. I think you would be a wonderful mother," he smiled, and then read the rectal thermometer he had removed from little Timmy who was lying there; still a little confused by the experience. "You are wonderful with children and that's always a plus."

There were four types of procedures she could choose from, one was called intracervical (in the cervical canal), and then there was, intrauterine (in the uterine cavity), and then the intrafollicular (in the ovarian follicle) and less we forget the intratubal (in the fallopian tubes).

All of the choices made her head swim as she reviewed them with Rashawn over dinner the night she had been given the green light to proceed.

"IUI is performed by passing a sterile catheter through the cervical canal into the uterine cavity and then injecting the sperm into the uterine cavity, which can be performed either by one of our fertility nurse practitioners on staff or by your own physician. The insemination procedure in itself causes little if any discomfort and following the insemination procedure the woman remains lying down with her hips elevated for forty-five minutes. Pregnancy rates average about fifteen to twenty percent per cycle," Rashawn read from the pamphlet. "Sounds like true love to me," she said mockingly. "Especially the hips in the air for forty-five minutes parts."

Qiana snatched the pamphlet from her.

"Stop! Are you still having that Superbowl party at your house at the end of the month?" she asked.

"Yes."

"Well, I wanna come," she said.

Rashawn almost choked on her raspberry tea.

"You? Ms. Party pooper of the century, oh my. What brings this on?"

"Well, I was at the clinic today and I picked out my '*baabee daadee*' and I could be pregnant from my first dose of him by Superbowl Sunday," she giggled as she felt her face grow hot. "Mr. Stock Market man. Black cap, right handed, big player in the market and he got really good grades in school. He's about six-foot and I really like his voice. He sounds like he has a cute and shy side."

"Wait let me get this straight, girlfriend; you get to hear their voices?" Rashawn grabbed Qiana's hand that kept her fork from taking the Alfredo to her mouth. "And what does 'black cap' mean?"

Qiana managed to fill her mouth with the food and then answered with it full.

"Lorraine said they categorize the races that way; black men-black cap, white men-white cap, etcetera. And yeah, I got to hear his voice, cool huh?"

"Forget the baby, that would make a cool dating service," Rashawn laughed. Qiana did too.

She had to admit it was actually comforting to sit in that cubicle listening to the different voices and reading the different profiles on the donors.

But when Lorraine had brought in the cassette for number 750, Qiana knew she liked him.

"I knew his profile would impress you but when you listen to his voice, man…you are gonna be like all in love with him. He sounds so shy and cute, ya know. I don't remember him or I'd tell you what he looks like. I wasn't working the day he came in." She looked around knowing that just the implication of doing what she had just suggested was against the rules. "It's been a couple of months and that was when we had that new girl, Mary. Anyway, I don't remember him, but it does say that he's a virgin."

"Pardon?" Qiana asked, sounding shocked. Lorraine shook her head.

"I don't mean *virgin*, virgin, I just mean that he has never impregnated before. It's like, so sweet; your first time, his first time."

"Lorraine you've been working here too long," Qiana said as she took the file and cassette from her. But as soon as she heard the man's voice she knew he was the one.

From his profile she was somewhat impressed but she knew for sure he would be the right donor for her, when she heard his voice. Though he didn't talk much about the stock market he filled her in on more personal things, his love for jazz and expensive cars and his voracity for authentic Italian food and expensive shoes.

He sounded so unsure of himself yet underneath there was an air of confidence. Qiana prided herself on learning a lot about people by the way they spoke. He was articulate and intelligent and she wanted that.

She would be adding to the next generation of African Americans and she wanted her son or daughter to be strong and intelligent, with no defect. And as number 750 spoke of his goals and dreams she knew he was to be the donor for her.

Lorraine winked as Qiana signed the form and wrote her check.

The day of the procedure had come; Qiana could barely wait to get home to tell Rashawn about it.

"So your legs were up in the air for forty five minutes. That sounds kinda fun," Rashawn laughed, as Qiana recanted the day's events to her.

Qiana tossed one of the small sofa pillows at Rashawn and then drew a different one up close to her, while she curled in the large recliner.

"Oh stop, it was my hips, not my legs."

"Have you told Rufus anything?"

"Now why would I do that? Why would I let him in my space? I stopped doing anything with him since before Christmas and the man hasn't even noticed. You'd think we were married."

"Are you scared to tell him?" Rashawn asked cautiously.

"No," Qiana answered with full confidence.

"Ok...So when will we know? I mean they're having a great sale at Baby World and I'm all ready to go," Rashawn sounded sincerely excited now.

"It'll be a while. I have to go back next month for them to do it again. But I swear, I know it's only been a day but I feel pregnant already."

"You are so cute," Rashawn smiled.

"Is the party still on?"

"Yes, 'Ms Party Animal.'"

Just then the door opened and Rufus entered the apartment. Rashawn notice Qiana's entire continence change. He smiled and kissed her forehead. She reached out to touch him but he had slid quickly from her reach.

"Where ya been?" she asked. He turned and made eye contact with Rashawn. She read the lie on his face before it came from his lips.

"Wit da ban…where else?" he said and then grinned. "I'll be washin' me butt and then getting owda ere, princess. Gotta be in the city tonight," he said, as he disappeared into the bathroom without much more conversation with the two women.

"See what I mean." Qiana gestured towards the sound of the running water. "Not even a 'Hey Rashe you gotta be gwon mon so I can be lovin me ol ladee," she mocked. "It's not like I've loved her in weeks." Qiana raised her soft voice slightly, knowing she still could not be heard above the water.

"Well I say get him out. Just kick him out." Rashawn stood and started for the bathroom door. "I say just open this door and go in there and kick his naked behind out. And say, 'don't let the back door hit cha where the good lord split cha roo fass," she yelled out the exaggerated name.

"Yeah mon," they heard him answer, and broke in to laughter.

CHAPTER 3

The excitement of the game was in the air. Nigel loved this day. He wagered heavily every year and always won. Even if it wasn't his favorite team playing, he seemed to always know who would win.

Sherry was going to refuse to join him today, as usual, but that was ok because this was the only time he was allowed, without a fight to say…'Ok, stay home and find something else to do, see ya' and leave.

It wasn't like the party was at their house and he would have to be sitting there, watching her pout because of not getting any attention. And by the time he got home she had usually recovered pretty well anyway. A day of calling her mother in Utah and talking with her for three or four hours, doing her nails, soaking in the tub, and eating chocolates—the really good kind; Nigel would dare to say it was her most favorite day of the year as well.

This year it was going to be at Terrell's girlfriend Rita's house. She lived clear across town with her sister but it was going to be worth the trip. Nigel had five hundred dollars riding on the Cowboys and they weren't going to let him down. He was never wrong.

He pulled on his Dallas Cowboys sweatshirt, not even bothering to straighten his hair, and tightened the laces of his ugliest pair of sneakers.

"Nigel," he heard Sherry call from the hall.

"Yeah sweetie. What's up? Gotta run. Whatcha need?" he answered, showing impatience in his voice.

"Well, I was just wondering," she said, following close behind him as he gathered up his wallet and keys. "I was wondering if I could go with?" she asked in a sweet voice that caused him to stop dead in his tracks.

"Go with? As in...with me?"

His eyes locked on his waiting Beamer parked out front. He hadn't even parked in the stall in the back last night so that this morning he could jump in and go. But now even *Brownie*, as he affectionately had named his car, seemed to overhear and cringe.

Qiana looked at herself in the mirror. She could have sworn she was glowing, even in that oversized Dallas Cowboys sweatshirt that she had borrowed from the side of the closet that belonged to Rufus, formally known as Russell, from his days when he used to enjoy a good football game. It seemed like a lifetime ago now.

"I still om tellin you mon, dat footbol game you be gwon to, spendin' ya hard earn money...for da white man...I don unerstan," he began, as he watched Qiana dress for the day.

He had just gotten home again after staying out for the last two nights, supposedly on some gig with his band. He was planning to leave again for two more weeks. He hadn't so much as called Qiana to check in since leaving the last time.

But what he hadn't known was that his life had check in on him in the form of a valley girl named Tracy, who called the house looking for him. She had checked in and had for some reason thought Qiana was his sister and inadvertently spilled the beans on their rendezvous over the last couple of months.

Qiana cut her eye at him and then continued to dress. She carefully applied her new lipstick. It was a great shade for her smooth caramel coloring. She wondered now how dark number 750's skin coloring was. He hadn't been very specific about his looks on the profile or on the cassette.

She hadn't had her period since the insertion over three weeks ago now, and was due for another insertion in a week. She had been told to expect her period a week later after the procedure. But it hadn't come. She had a feeling she was pregnant already.

The doctor had warned her that she might see some changes in her cycle. And he added in his explanation of what to expect that she should not to let those changes overly excite her, as often the body would react strangely to invasion such as an intercervical procedure. But Qiana knew it was more than just a simple change in her cycle. She could just tell.

"You are lookin' very different today my lady," Rufus said, moving up close behind her. He moved his hands around her waist and squeezed slightly. She moved his arms from around her and turned to look at him. She looked deep into his brown eyes.

"Nope," was all she said. His face became covered with an expression of confusion.

"Nope what?" he asked.

"Nope, I'm not gonna let you do anything to me. Not touch me, not anything." She smiled and went back to her mirror to make sure that all of her braids are all up in the scrungie. She wanted to look casual yet neat. She was always neat; it was part of her job to look crisp and neat.

Today, she would try to let her hair down just a little, not much, but a little.

Today she wanted to end it with Rufus.

She knew she should have taken care of it months ago. Perhaps she was holding onto him in case the implant didn't work. Perhaps…

"I got a call from Tracy," Qiana said calmly without looking at him. She could feel the air tighten around them.

"Oh, Tracy uh…she is uh…" he began.

"She is your lover and I am your sister," she continued as she tightened the scrungie a little more, by pulling the braids through.

"Qiana, baby." He started for her, but she turned to him quickly before he could touch her.

"Yes, Russell?" she asked sarcastically.

He blinked tightly as if trying to metamorphous back into the man he once was.

"What does she have that I don't have?" Qiana asked. "Never mind, I don't want to know. I guess what gets me, is that you criticize me for working for 'de white man'. You get all over me because I have white friends and I don't use Ebonics at work and I try to rise above the stereotypes and then you…You go behind my back and do this…and with a white woman. But then, I guess I have a secret too," she smiled, feeling suddenly very self-confident.

"And what is that Qiana, you've found someone else? I'm not going to make any excuses for Tracy; she's a nothing in my life; just a little groupie looking for a jolly but you…You are my life. Please don't tell me you found someone else, because I will only feel like you did it out of spite. I would hate to see you hurting yourself out of spite." He sat on the bed. His eyes began to fill with tears. She held out her hand.

"Don't even do that Russ. Don't even try to sit there and cry. Get up and get your stuff and get out. Oh, except for this sweatshirt. I kinda like it and I'm on my way to a Superbowl party with my friends." She smacked her lips, feeling her neck jerk just a little.

"I can't get out, I don't have anyplace else to go."

"Go to Tracy."

"Don't start that. Get over it-ok. I admitted it. I didn't deny it."

"Look I've got to dash, but when I get back you be outty, ok?" she said in a perky tone remembering how Tracy sounded on the phone; perky, like most of the nineteen or twenty year old cheerleader types from the valley. She couldn't have been much older than that.

Qiana started out the room only to have Russell grab her arm tightly.

"I know you don't plan any violence, Russ." Qiana's fist tightened as all the resentment and anger she had been holding in since the call from Tracy began to surface. They stared deep in each other eyes for a moment as if both in deep contemplation over the next move either would make. Russell then loosened his grip on her arm, letting out a nervous chuckle.

"Man Qi, if I didn't know you any better, I'd say you were getting ready to bust me up a little bit," he chuckled. "When did you get so aggressive? I guess not getting any for so long makes women kinda mean," he added. Qiana rolled her eyes and walked out of the room.

"Leave your key in the mailbox, Russell." That was the last thing he heard her say as the door closed behind her.

She sang loudly to the cranked up radio as she drove to Rashawn's. She felt free and happy and complete.

The Palemos was a small community that had made itself a town unto itself. Though it was just across town from Redwood City, you knew the minute you had crossed over into it.

A track of no more than three city blocks of houses and a narrow strip mall that consisted of a Sally's Deli, a liquor store slash laundry mat and a video rental, made up the bulk of this community. The houses were all quaint and of equal size, about fifteen hundred square feet. They all had yards with chain linked or picket fences and mature trees. The area lent itself to the homey feel of family and Nigel wanted to wager that Rita and her family owned most of it…with squatter's rights, if nothing else. He would always hear her say, "*My aunt around the corner, or cousin Jody over there…*" It wasn't a ghetto by any means, though many of the inhabitants appeared of middle to low-income range, retired seniors, and families with lots of children. All the yards were well cared for and clean, as were the streets, though many cars lined them. They ranged in all values, from the green Pinto, that had never moved since the communities founding, no doubt, to the shiny red Corvette that was Nigel's favorite. He knew it to belong to Rita's sister, Rashawn.

He had a couple of clients from *The Palemos*; he was trying now to bring back their names to his memory as they stood on Rita's porch ringing the bell. The neighbor, an elderly black woman without her teeth in, opened her screen and peeked out. He smiled and nodded his cap at her. Feeling Sherry's grip tighten on his arm, even without even looking at her, he could tell she was uncomfortable already. He noticed Terrell's car; a shiny little blue convertible Porsche parked up the block.

Parking had been tight on the street. He had to park around the corner.

"They're in there, you just gotta knock loud. Wit all dat racket theys keepin' up in there," the woman said, speaking loudly.

"Oh my Gawd," Sherry sighed. "She must be neighborhood watch. I really hate nosy neighbors," she breathed heavily.

Just then the door flew open. It was a woman that Nigel didn't recognize. She looked a lot like Rita; only she wore long extended braids with gold shimmering threads going through them. Her nails were cut short and neat and she wore no polish.

"You must be T's man, Nyge, and his blonde chick, we were expecting you," the woman said and then laughed out loud. It was clear she had had a couple of drinks and was feeling no pain. Nigel immediately wanted some of what she had. She stepped out on the porch. "It's ok, auntie, they are our friends. We are having a Superbowl party."

She spoke deliberately slow and louder than need be, almost in a taunting fashion, to the seeming quick-witted older woman.

"Want I should bring you some beer or something?" she yelled. The older woman responded with a toothless grin and then fanned her hand at her and went back inside. The woman at the door looked at Nigel and shrugged her shoulders. "I guess that means yes," she smiled. She had to be one of Rita's sisters. Nigel noticed she was just as pretty as he had always found Rita to be.

Rita had three or four sisters, but he had only met one…Rashawn.

Inside the volume grew at least thirty decibels from the porch. The music, the TV, the cheering and the laughter, it was a party all right, complete, of course, with Smithy, their old friend from law school who, for the life of him, couldn't pass the bar, and Luis.

This would be Luis' first year joining them. He was a new with the firm and wanted very badly to fit in. He was a Hispanic man from down south, LA way. He had just moved here with his family when invited to join the firm. Dave was trying to make sure the firm's associate staff was diverse and was accomplishing it by taking on new attorneys from all over.

Unlike when his father ran the show; there was only Lydia, his secretary, still the firm's only secretary. Now for diversity there was Terrell the African American, Norm the Jewish guy, Luis the Hispanic and lest we not forget, Nigel, being of Italian descent behind that blonde hair and those hazel eyes of his.

Nigel had always wished he had gone by his mother's maiden name of Costillano. At least that sounded more Italian than Godwins and it sure would have eliminated much confusion over his ethnicity. He never understood how his Italian father could have a name like Nigel Godwins. But his grandfather always would explain it had something to do with Sicily back in 1910…and then he would start to cry. Nigel never did get the full understanding of that one, but Nigel Godwins it was, and he was Italian…so take it or leave it.

"Hey man, just in time!" Terrell yelled from over the full house.

Most of the people there were friends of Rita and Terrell's. Nigel found out later the woman at the door was indeed one of Rita's sisters, the one that was called the *real* doctor, Ta'Rae…as opposed to Rashawn, the *fake doctor*, as they affectionately call her.

Before long, Ta'Rae's pager sounded and she was immediately transformed into a serious, sober professional. Excusing herself cordially, she left the party.

Even with a house full of lawyers and doctors, fake or otherwise, Sherry was no more comfortable with the crowd. Everyone was loud and rambunctious-far from the professionals they normally were-and she was being totally ignored. She regretted that curiosity had gotten the better of her.

The wanting to know every part of Nigel's life definitely had its pit-
falls. Even the night she had met his family. Meeting his mother was fine
and maybe even his grandmother, but that grandfather of his...he
hated her immediately. It had been a disastrous evening that she had
gotten herself trapped into...sort of like this one was turning out to be.

Soon she found herself in the kitchen, basically hiding out. It was a
surprisingly a quiet place without a lot of traffic. She wondered if anyone would notice if she made a phone call. *She felt driven to it.*

When all was said and done she had planned to blame Nigel for the
whole affair anyway. His neglect, his lack of caring for her needs and
lately, he was just plain non-loving...that's why she had started seeing
James outside of work.

James worked for her father, he had hired him in a lateral position to
her own and that was exciting. She had never had any competition on
her job before. Whatever she did was A-OK with daddy and then suddenly, there was James.

She hated him in the beginning and would complain to Nigel every
night about him. But then suddenly about a month or two ago something changed. She and James were working late one evening and
decided to call a truce from another day of bickering. They were
nowhere near finished working for the day so they decided to order dinner in. It was there, over the potato salad and hot wings, they found out
everything in common that they shared. Both had family in Utah, both
loved children; both regretted seeing the *Gilligan's Island* show can-
celled. They laughed for hours; so many hours in fact that Sherry didn't
get home until after midnight. Nigel was fast asleep and never seemed
to have noticed.

"Hello James," Sherry whispered into the phone.

Back in the living room, Qiana knew she was shocking Rashawn to
pieces with her involvement in the game. She was being loud and crude
and loving it. Everyone was crowded around the giant screen TV, sitting
around on the floor eating potato chips and sub sandwiches. She too

was throwing popcorn when the *'wrong calls'* were made, along with everyone else.

She decided for the first time she wasn't going to stand out. She wasn't going to be a wallflower. Maybe it was just a hormone imbalance, but she felt great, empowered even.

It was the second half of the game but even before the winning touchdown Qiana began to sense victory. And as player crossed the goal line, she began to pound Nigel's shoulder relentlessly, as if playing a bongo drum.

It didn't hurt but Nigel did notice her. She had a cute round face; one that didn't need make up to be considered pretty. It made him smile just watching her enjoying herself. Her voice was one that he could tell wasn't used to yelling, as she could barely be heard above the rest of the room. Her hands were small and her nails were immaculate and well manicured. He assumed she might also be one of the doctors there. Suddenly, she noticed he was noticing her, pounding on his shoulder. She stopped abruptly and he could almost see the blush come up under her smooth brown cheeks. The cheering consumed the room and popcorn flew as they locked eyes on each other for just a second. She suddenly jumped up and moved quickly away from him and disappeared into one of the rooms.

Rashawn noticed Qiana moving quickly into the bedroom. She followed.

"What's wrong?" Rashawn asked as Qiana flopped onto the bed with her face in her hands.

"Oh, my god, I was out there beating the devil out of that guy," she giggled. Rashawn sighed, relieved.

"Oh, I thought you were sick. All that jumping around and screaming you're doing out there…"

"Is it bad for the baby?"

"He might go deaf. Wait a minute, what baby?" Rashawn asked, trying to clear her foggy mind to concentrate on what could be serious conversation. She wasn't much of a drinker and had reached her limit with just two beers.

"I know I'm pregnant. I just know it."

"Maybe not Qi, don't get too carried away. These things take time. Remember I'm a doctor, I know these things."

"You have a doctorate. You're a teacher," Qiana said putting her hands on Rashawn's shoulder in mock consolation.

"Oh, I always get confused because they call me Doctor Maxwell at the school," she mocked serious confusion. "So did 'roof roof' ever come home, mon? And what did ja do bout da white woman mon?" Rashawn asked, mocking what she knew to be Rufus' fake Jamaican accent. Qiana suddenly remembered the confrontation earlier that day and reached for the phone.

"I kicked his ass to the curb, dat's what, mon," she said coolly. Rashawn was suddenly very sober.

"You what? You fired Russell after all these years? The man you could never say no to, always forgiving, Russell? The, bust me upside my head, I like it, do it again, Russell?"

"Yes, and I need to call and make sure he's gone. I don't even want him there when I get home," she remarked as she picked up the phone, only to hear…

"*Oh yes, James, I think I can get away. Nigel isn't suspecting a thing…hold on. I think someone is on the other end,*" when she picked up the line. She hung up quickly.

"What was that?"

"I don't know but I think somebody is plotting something against somebody named Niles," Qiana said. Rashawn thought for a moment but couldn't jog her memory to connect with the name.

Qiana picked up the phone again and the line was free so she called her apartment, there was no answer. Russell had left. Suddenly Qiana wasn't sure at all, how she was feeling. She hung up, as her own voice on the answering machine could be heard.

"What's wrong?"

"Rufus is gone," Qiana said as she felt tears welling up. She couldn't stop them and began to cry. Rashawn put her arms around her shoulders to comfort her.

It wasn't long before the TV went off and the stereo went on again. Many of the guests had left. The few remaining, were getting comfortable as Rita straightened up some of the clutter and food remains.

Nigel had found out indirectly his error in thinking that, Rita's sister, Rashawn was an actual medical doctor. She was a professor at UC Santa Clara. Doctor Rashawn Maxwell was her professional title but...

"It just doesn't mean the same once said in context. Ta'Rae is the only 'real' doctor here," Nigel remarked frankly.

"Oh, so now I'm nobody," Rashawn teased as Nigel blushed, from once again saying the wrong thing.

"No, it just means he wouldn't want you giving him a vasectomy, Shawn," Terrell laughed out loud. Nigel's face was on fire now.

"I feel like you already have," he mumbled under his breath.

"Ok, let's see what we all do here so we can get everything out in the open. I'm the noblest of all here for I be a teacher. Rita, in there cleaning up, is the maid..." Rashawn laughed.

"And what do you do?" Sherry asked Qiana who had found her a quiet spot in the corner as she reverted back to her normal self. Since the phone call she felt instantly deflated.

"Oh, I'm a pediatric nurse," she said as she sipped her juice. Sherry tried to look impressed but it was forced and Qiana could tell. "And you?"

"Oh, I own Cruxtonoden Construction. We manufacture prefab housing. Our base is Utah, but we have a company right over in Campbell," she said showing her proud side without abasement.

Nigel glanced over at her as he had only heard the 'own' part of her statement. She was talking to the on-his-shoulder-bongo-playing round-faced woman. Deep inside Nigel was hoping she had been the real Doctor there. He didn't know why he wanted Sherry to feel unimportant but he just did.

Rita offered Sherry a glass of wine. Nigel noticed her eyebrow rise slightly as she saw that the crystal wineglass resembled their set at home. He wanted to say out loud…

'Yes, Sherry, lots of people use expensive crystal and they drink the good stuff too. Not just us.'

He didn't have any idea why he was feeling so hostile towards her tonight; he just was. Perhaps it was the fact that he was just now seeing her for the first time all evening. Where had she been? First she intrudes on his day and then disappears, only to reappear and start sounding pompous around his friends.

That was it…he was feeling guilty.

He knew it now. He was angry with Sherry for no good reason. It had to be the *Family Makers Sperm Bank* visit that was on is agenda for tomorrow that had him instantly uptight. Here he had, in his mind, just accused Sherry of everything from racism to snobbery…next he'd think she was having and affair. The thought made him chuckle to himself.

He had told Dave he wouldn't be in because he had something very personal to tend to. Dave assuming it had to do with Sherry gave him a wink. If only he knew it was as far from Sherry as he could get.

He had never reneged on anything before in his life. But Terrell had convinced him to get back his donation and that this would be for the best. He had to agree.

"Oh yes, I want a house full of children," Sherry could be heard saying now to the round faced woman. Nigel once again mentally joined the group. He could feel Terrell's eyes burning a whole in the side of his head. Nigel finally looked at him as his eyes darted to and fro towards Sherry. Suddenly Rita hunched him hard.

"What choo buggin' yo eyes at Nyge for. I wanna baybee too," she said leaning her body up close into his.

"You don't even need no baby, you got me, gurl," Terrell said and kissed her quickly—more of a peck actually. There was laughter all around.

"Well, I, for my part, ain't father material," Nigel said as he stood and stretched. "And I have a long day tomorrow, we better go."

"You still taking that personal?" Luis asked.

Nigel was caught mid-stretch as he froze with eyes locked on Terrell who now cleared his throat. The air grew thick.

"What personal? We doing something tomorrow, sweetie?" Sherry spoke up sounding truly sincere.

Qiana watched both guilty faces; the woman who was apparently the one on the phone making a plan with someone named James and here was the Niles or Nigel, rather…part of the conversation with secret plans of his own. They were a pair to bet all pairs, she thought to herself as she was hit again with the reality of Russell's unfaithfulness.

"Ah yeah. I was plannin' a surprise for us baby and my man Luis just like, blew it," he said glaring at him. Luis's wife Maria slapped his arm.

"See, you're blowin' it man. You ain't gon get no friends at this rate," Maria said, as she too laughed along with everyone else. Luis apologized profusely. No one seemed to notice the beads of sweat that had immediately come to Nigel's forehead. No one seemed to notice Sherry, biting her lip in complex thought on how she would get her plans with James changed…No one that is, except for Qiana.

Nigel had won a thousand dollars that night. No one would have guessed it by the quiet ride he and Sherry had going back across to Redwood City.

They went into the back of their condo and on into the stall, without saying anything.

Nigel pulled on his sweat pants and climbed into bed. His mind soared in a thousand different directions. What was the big deal anyway? He could just tell Sherry what he did? She would understand. He would tell her tomorrow, after he explained to the *Family Makers* clinic that he accidentally forgot to mention that he was merely storing his specimen and they were not for implantation…

'Why did you make the tape then buster?' she would ask.

'Oh the tape? Uh I thought it was part of the rules', he would simply answer.

'Part of the rules? What kind of a lawyer talks like that? What kind of a lawyer thinks like that?' he sighed.

Sherry climbed into bed next to him. Tonight she moved close to him, closer than she had in weeks. He looked deep into her blue eyes.

"Nigel, I want a baby," she said. He blinked slowly. "Now I don't know what you had planned for us for tomorrow and I think it's sweet and all but, hear this: unless it was a romantic retreat we need to cancel it to stay home and make a baby," she said. Her normally soft voice was cool and austere.

"It doesn't happen like that Sherry," Nigel responded flatly.

"Why not? If I can take my temperature every morning, and tell myself I am now spontaneously in the mood to conceive, you can at least try to be part of the effort."

"I didn't know you were taking your temperature every morning and I sure didn't know there had been effort."

"Why do you think I haven't done anything with you in weeks? I was trying to conserve you."

"Conserve me?" Nigel sat up.

"Yes. The book says that if a man doesn't ejaculate too much before the woman is ready to conceive that when the time comes and her temperature is ready she can conceive and probably have a boy." Sherry was beginning to sound all too sincere. It was scaring him. He climbed quickly out of bed. "This morning I was ready so I think we should have sex now."

"Sherry I think you…" Nigel paused. "I think you're serious aren't you? You read a book and now…" Nigel stood stunned for a second before walking out of the bedroom and into the kitchen. He poured himself a brandy and gulped it down. He was trying to understand what was happening to him. It suddenly was very confusing.

How could it have been so easy for him to become a father through anonymous donation yet the woman he was suppose to love was now begging to become mother to his seed and he was refusing. He hated himself. When had he become so uncaring? He was now officially what could be called…a heel.

He walked back to bedroom but went only as far as the doorway. He just knew he would find Sherry crying. Instead, she was still sitting in the bed, with arms folded tight across her chest.

"Sherry, I have something I have to do tomorrow. I…" he began. Her daunting glare became suddenly too much. He waved his hand in surrender and moved on past the bedroom to sleep on the sofa in the spare room.

CHAPTER 4

Qiana had planned on lunch with Lorraine, the day after the Superbowl, and had agreed to meet her at *Family Makers*. She had gotten there around eleven still dressed in her smock and nurse's whites.

It was still a bit early so she thought she would just cruise the halls and get comfortable with her now, most favorite place in the world.

She knew it was a psychological attachment she was feeling towards this facility, but it didn't matter. She just loved the *Family Makers Sperm Bank*. The entire staff there was just so friendly and supportive. And that Lorraine, she really knew her stuff. Everyone she saw come in was smiling.

Except Nigel Godwins, that is.

Qiana could not believe her eyes when she saw him come through the glass doors. He strolled in trying to look nonchalant in that staunch dark suit, topcoat and alligator shoes, but it wasn't working. She could tell he was very uncomfortable. Qiana wanted so badly to hear what was going on when he approached the counter, but within seconds it seemed; he was being shown into the administrator's office.

Perhaps he was going to donate? Perhaps he was here to pick up his storage, so that he and that pretty little girlfriend of his could start their family. They would surely have some beautiful children. He was very handsome and her eyes were a lovely shade of blue. They didn't seem in love but then no one was really here for love's sake. What did love really have to do with making a baby? Suddenly, she stopped herself in mid thought and had to shake her head...she had a lot of nerve.

If she were so sure of herself and her convictions that love and a relationship were not expected for a person considering a family, she would have told her mother and father by now of her intent to get artificially inseminated. But she hadn't even told them she and Russell had broken up. She knew she needed back up, in case she needed to pin her baby on someone, some real person. Russell would be as easy a blame as any body.

Looking at it from that angle, maybe she was right. Maybe love didn't have too much to do with this, because she sure didn't love Russell...not anymore.

Suddenly, she could hear voices through the wall behind her head. They were talking kind of loud, and though she hadn't meant to eavesdrop, she could hear everything.

"What do you mean there has been a mix up? This is so unacceptable...I am being calm! I just want my...my sperm back. Oh, this is so unacceptable!" she heard the man say. She realized then, she knew that voice. She had heard it recently. She knew it had to be the friend of Terrell's, she had seen him go in. But it was even more familiar to her than even that. Through the wall he sounded more and more like the voice she had heard on the cassette.

Just then she saw Lorraine coming towards her, with a face stiff with mortification.

"What's wrong?" Qiana asked, in a half whisper.

"I am so sorry, we are going to have to cancel lunch. We are about to get sued! I just feel it," she whispered.

"By that guy that just came in?" Qiana pointed towards the office she saw Nigel go into. Lorraine nodded.

"He came to get his specimen and we can't find it," Lorraine said. She was sounding nervous and Qiana felt terrible for her.

"What could have happened?"

"I don't know. But in just the little time since he called this morning, I looked through the files where he should have been and he wasn't there. He had to have come in when we had this temp working here, Mary. Oh my Gawd, did she ever turn out to be a real zinger."

"I don't want to hear this Lorraine." Qiana began to get worried about her own case.

"Oh no, it wouldn't have affected you. I don't think," Lorraine said, not making full eye contact, as she heard Nigel ranting through the thin wall.

"Besides, you are probably not even pregnant. And we will just start you over with files from after the first of the year," Lorraine said and walked away.

The door flew open and Nigel stormed out. Qiana sat back close to the wall and pulled her magazine up to her face.

"Seven-o-five," he snapped. "Seven-o-five," he repeated.

Lorraine's voice could be heard now.

"I can hear you sir, you don't have to yell at me. I'm not the one who filed your specimen. Now, here in seven-o-five is your profile, correct?" There was a silence as Qiana peeked from behind the magazine to see Nigel looking through some papers.

"Yes this is me."

"But you see your specimen is not here, in here is specimen seven-five-o, you see, and it has a black cap. Your cassette isn't in here neither, this cassette says seven-five-o." Lorraine paused. "Let me check something," she said, as Nigel began to pace. Qiana once again raised the magazine as she thought he might look her way.

"Oh my, here's your cassette and your specimen in drawer seven-fifty, see here, and the profile, seven fifty is in here with your specimen-seven-o-five. And I'm afraid there are only two more vials left in here with the dates you mentioned. Oh my Gawd, it has a black cap on it too and one is gone."

Qiana could not believe her ears. If what she was hearing…was what she was hearing! *'She was pregnant with Nigel's baby. The specimen she had been implanted with was labeled seven-o-five'* she was instantly upset.

Wait! Maybe she wasn't pregnant at all; she began to think, trying to hold off the panic attack that was forming. Everyone had said it couldn't happen this soon. *She had only had one implantation. Maybe-just maybe, there really had been no mistake and she had been give Mr. Stock Market instead of Mr. Lawyer. Mr. non-black, 'I don't want nothin' to do with a baby', lawyer.* She began to feel as if she would hyperventilate…She needed air but was afraid to move from behind her magazine for fear Nigel would see her.

She hadn't specified on paper that it was exclusively a black man she wanted, *but Lorraine knew that! She knew she wanted a black baby. When she handed her Mr. Black Stock Market man's profile she knew…*But it had been Nigel's voice on that cassette Qiara heard…and his sperm donation she had been inseminated with…

Her throat was getting dry and she was having a hard time swallowing. She once again peeked at Nigel.

There he was, standing there…*clearly under six-foot tall, blonde and…that nose of his…much too large for her taste. What was Lorraine thinking!* Qiana began to think irrationally, as if Lorraine had done this on purpose…as if she had done anything at all!

"Look, I'm going to leave and discuss this with my colleagues and see if I should pursue this matter with legal means," Nigel said, trying to regain his composure.

"I'm very sorry Mr. Godwins, but I'm looking at your original contract here and you also didn't stipulate that you didn't want your sperm dispersed. You didn't pay a storage fee or sign a maintenance agreement so we could safely assume it was ok to…" Lorraine patiently began to explain the policy on non-delegated specimens.

"Perhaps you didn't understand the contract. Perhaps you should have discussed it with your attorney," she finished up by saying; sarcasm was in her tone now. About that moment Nigel stormed out.

Qiana waited for a few more minutes and then slowly approached the counter. Lorraine and apparently her supervising administrator were discussing their possible options if Nigel were to find a way sue them. Lorraine spun around and smiled overly wide at Qiana.

"Lorraine, may I have a word with you?" she said softly. The administrator nodded and Lorraine stepped from behind the counter, to join Qiana in a stroll outside.

After they had walked for a few steps, Qiana spoke.

"Lorraine, I'm sure I wasn't suppose to hear anything that was said in there," she began speaking slowly, as Lorraine shook her head.

"It's a mess. We kinda knew there had been a mix up but no one had come in to get their sperm back yet so, we just thought we could get it all straightened out before anyone figured anything out; it's not too many files anyway."

"Can he do that, sue I mean?"

"Well, not really. He didn't even read the small print. You can't just leave a specimen here without telling us what to do with it. I wasn't here the day he came in so I just figured his papers were filled out correctly. So when he came back to leave a specimen the next week, I didn't ask anything special about his contract. Why would I, it was Mary's case file. He didn't care about his sperm. And I don't think he really cares now. He's just mad that he didn't know something. I'm more concerned about some of the other clients that Mary mixed up. I guess she was a little dyslexic," Lorraine chuckled nervously. "We didn't know until it was too late. She's been let go."

"Lorraine," Qiana paused. "I heard him tell you his number was seven five-o. But if seven-o-five was in the drawer for seven five-o…well, that's the tray that the nurse had brought in for me. I looked real close at the tray number. Not the vial itself but the tray did say seven five-o," she said in a tone that demanded a reply, though it wasn't a question. Lorraine stopped and stared deep into Qiana's soft brown eyes.

"Oh honey, I'm so sorry. But chances are you aren't even pregnant and we can just start over with another group," she said sounding deeply and truly sincere. "I mean, we can give you the real seven fifty now if you want."

"I feel sorta funny, ya know." Qiana chuckled after a second or two of assimilating Lorraine's words. "I feel like I just cheated with him. I know that guy, number seven-o-five," Qiana admitted.

"You do?" Lorraine's voice rose to a new high. "That's not the way it was suppose to happen? You are never supposed to meet the donor."

"And I know his girlfriend. She sure wants his baby more than I do. I feel like a thief."

"Oh sweetie, don't. It was that crazy backward Mary's fault and besides, he came here of his own free will and he didn't say he was saving those few vials for anybody in particular. We have forms for that and he didn't fill one out. He didn't leave enough to make this big of a stink over anyway," Lorraine consoled.

"Now you just go on home and wait for your period and then give us a call for your next appointment. I have to make some...." Lorraine looked back in the direction of he clinic and sighed heavily, "calls."

Qiana didn't know which person she felt worse for as she drove back to work, Nigel, Sherry, Lorraine or herself.

CHAPTER 5

Nigel knew it would be a far stretch to say he was on his best behavior, but what else could he attempt, but being polite, as Sherry's friends began to fill the condo.

Mark, the owner of a mid town travel agency, and one of Sherry's male friends, seemed to notice him hiding out in the kitchen, trying to stay out of everyone's way.

"Hey there, Goodwin," Mark said with that plastic smile of his and outstretched hand. Nigel strained a smile and nodded.

"Godwins," he corrected, as he shook his hand. Mark blushed slightly.

"Sorry, I always seem to make that mistake," he chuckled. "What is that, Jewish?" he chuckled nervously.

"Nope, still Italian, Mark," Nigel said, trying to keep the bite out of his tone. Mark nodded in full acknowledgment of the reprimand. This had only been about the twelfth time they had had this conversation.

"So Sherry tells me that you and her are planning a trip to the Caribbean," he added. Nigel checked the alcohol level of his glass, trying not to show his surprise at the comment.

"Hmm…planned? Sure," he mumbled and then turned the snifter up, draining it. Mark cleared his throat.

"Oh, perhaps I spilled the beans," Mark added, with another nervous chuckle. Nigel refilled his Brandy snifter and then held out the carafe towards Mark's glass. He covered the mouth of it his glass with his palm.

"Uh no…mineral water," he smiled. Nigel nodded and again turned up his glass, emptying it with one gulp.

"What about that Superbowl?" Nigel then asked, attempting conversation. Mark's face grimaced slightly.

"No sports," he said.

The two men stood silent for a moment and then Mark sighed loudly and looked at his Rolex.

"Well, I would think everyone is here, so perhaps we should get back in the living room so we don't appear rude." He once again planted on his plastic smile.

"Ahh…rude, can't be rude," Nigel agreed.

The living room scene was no better, as some were deeply involved in half-whispered gossip and fake laughter, others on topics that were nowhere near Nigel's area of interest.

"I had to take my pedigree in for grooming last week and she was more than just a little upset at her cut," a woman named Simone said, in full voice. Nigel hadn't been paying too much attention to any of them but that comment brought him quickly back to the now.

"I wonder how difficult it would be to sue them?" she asked, directing her question to Nigel. At that moment, Nigel began to regret every ounce of alcohol he had consumed since arriving home, for he could now feel the wide goofy grin on his face that, for the life of him, could not be removed.

As the room seemed to grow quiet, everyone's eyes were on him; Sherry's included; only hers tightened, letting him know she was on alert and prepared for purgation of whatever he might say…at a moment's notice.

Nigel knew his choices were limited now. He could end the evening with just a few choice words…or, he could be a good boy and say the right thing…the power he held made his head swim.

He had to reason, which response would benefit him *after* the crowd had gone. He stared deep into Sherry's eyes; that were now pleading for him to choose the latter.

"Well, Simone, one my associates at the firm would be glad to take a consultation with you. I'm afraid my specialty lies in the domestic department…like say your dog was beating you…now then I would have some answers for you," Nigel said, sounding all together serious.

There was a moment of silence and then a sharp burst of laughter. Nigel had been saved. By his own wit he now could make it through this evening without saying another word and still be considered Sherry's charming man-friend.

"The dog beating her?" Sherry chuckled as she climbed into bed.

"Why didn't you invite James?" Nigel asked without any deep thought, as he climbed into bed as well.

"Why would I invite him?" Sherry answered in a sharp tone.

"Oh, I dunno, I guess because I thought you had once said you wanted to maybe get, 'James the charmless' and 'Simone the brainless', together."

"Don't be so rude. You were very rude tonight, I just want to tell you that," she added and then clicked off the lamp, putting them in the dark.

"Rude? Oh please, I was great I've never been better," he remarked snidely and then groped for her.

"Not tonight, I have a headache," she said flatly.

"A headache? What's up with that?" he laughed sardonically. "Funny how you never get a headache until you've spent an evening with those people," Nigel said towards what he knew to be her back, even in the dark.

"Those people?" she began, sitting up quickly in the bed. Nigel groaned out loud at what he knew to be the start of an argument.

"Oh my god…look, I'm sorry. I'm sorry. Let's kiss and make up." He leaned over to kiss her. She pushed away his advance.

"Let's settle it tonight. I hate your friends you hate my friends, period!" she snapped, slamming her arms across her chest.

"Ok, and I hate you and you hate me; let's make out," he continued on, in a playful manner.

"You just don't get it do you?" she sighed. "Nigel, you are going to have to wake up and realize what world you are living in. Your friends are not going to help your upward mobility. They aren't going to do a thing for your career. They are literal drags. They are holding you back from being a success. They are so unprofessional. They would never and I mean never help you out in any way what so ever. They take, take, and take, and I mean emotionally. My friends give, they empower me, not drain me."

"You're serious aren't you? Did you read that in a book too?" he asked. "You're right, Sherry, I hate your friends...even more now. Mostly because you believe that they could possibly represent the real world. She wants to *sue* her *groomer* because her *dog* doesn't like his cut...oh paalease! Not to sound dramatic, but Terrell is my best friend and I would do anything for him," he said and turned his back to her.

He lay quiet hoping she would believe he could possibly sleep after what she had just said.

"Yeah well...under all your joking around...is just more joking around," she said with a sneer in her voice.

The next morning Nigel still had residual disturbance from the conversation with Sherry the night before.

"Terrell, do you think I'm not serious enough?" he asked Terrell as they rode the elevator of the courthouse together.

"Nigel if you were any more serious you'd be a corpse," Terrell said, without cracking a smile. He had a difficult case later today and wasn't in a joking mood.

"Thanks," Nigel said, shaking his hand. Terrell nodded, as they both existed onto the fourth floor.

Outside room forty awaited Nigel's client, Mrs. Burke. She was a woman in her late forties though, due to abuses from her husband, she looked much older. Her eldest son had forced her to pursue the divorce from her husband. He had explained to Nigel that his father had been a vicious pig and his mother deserved better treatment, so he had convinced her to divorce him and sue for alimony and child support for the remaining three of the eight children living at home.

Her soft blue eyes danced nervously now as she spoke.

"Mr. Godwins, I've changed my mind. I've decided not to go through with this."

"What are you talking about?" Nigel asked as he let the door to the courtroom close behind Terrell who had gone in ahead of him.

This case was only going to take a few minutes as they were early on the courts docket, and Mr. Burke had defaulted. Terrell and Nigel were going to take in breakfast and discuss the heavier case Terrell had on the docket for the afternoon. This was a cakewalk...

"Mrs. Burke, have you been threatened?" Nigel asked cautiously, as he moved her away from the courtroom entrance and over towards the window. Out of the corner of his eye he noticed Terrell stepping back out of the courtroom.

He was about to tell him that Judge Cox had just entered, but before the words could clear his lips, he saw the man stepping from the unguarded elevator and then the glistening of the pistol.

All Nigel heard was his name being called out, before Terrell, taking Mrs. Burke with them; tackled him to the ground on top of her, shielding them both from the flying bullets.

Screams and other sounds of panic were heard now.

Before anyone could focus completely on the fact that the assailant was no other than Mr. Burke, he had been apprehended.

Mrs. Burke lay face down with her hands covering her ears, shaking. Nigel turned to see Terrell who was examining himself for possible gunshot wounds. Their eyes met, and immediately his words to Sherry, spoken just the night before, filled his thoughts...and he knew now, Terrell would do anything for him as well.

CHAPTER 6

Qiana reached her apartment only to find Russell waiting out front of the building. Not Rufus, but Russell, dressed in black jeans and a burgundy sweater. It was the sweater that her mother had bought him for Christmas last year. She didn't think he still had it or would dare be seen in such a preppy looking thing. It looked nice on him, just like she had imagined it would. *He looked nice.* His hair was cut close to his head and his face was smooth from a fresh shave.

She checked her mail trying to ignore him, while she calmed her heart. He hadn't looked this good since the day they had met.

The day they met he was touring the hospital with the group of young interns from Stanford. He was in the biochemistry program. He was in that program to get a leg up for a position opening in the lab where he worked.

"I wanted to get more hands on experience," he had said.

Qiana wasn't really listening to him over that small bistro table, as he wined and dined her. She had gotten too caught up in his eyes.

Within three months he had moved in and within a year he had dropped out of school and the rest was history.

"Qiana, these are for you, my lady, happy birthday," he said, pulling a small bouquet of yellow roses from behind his back. Her heart leapt. She almost had to hold it in. Though she tried to hide the smile, it was there, wide and bright.

Opening the door she walked in with him following. They didn't say much to each other as she removed her jacket and hung it in the closet, loosened her braids and shook them. She put the flowers in a vase and started the teakettle. Taking down a cup, she suddenly remembered he was in the living room and pulled down another.

She had gotten used to being totally alone over the last month and half. It hadn't been too far off from the way it had become anyway, only now she hadn't been waiting for his return.

"I really wanted to talk to you," he called from the living room. "I've been thinking a lot about us. I'm speaking of the permanent us," he said.

She immediately began to think about what she would say. What she would do? Today, her pregnancy had been confirmed a second time by a blood test. No one could believe that she had actually been impregnated on her first implantation.

She had been given the option to reconsider going through with this pregnancy...under the circumstances they understood. But today she gave them her final decision; she would keep this baby-even under the circumstances.

"Where have you been staying?" Qiana asked as she put the two tea-spoons of sugar in his cup. There was a long silence.

"With my brother," he finally answered. Qiana sighed, as she only half believed him. Russell hadn't spoken to his brother in over a year.

She took the two cups of tea back with her in to the living room, where he had made himself comfortable on the sofa. She sat across from him in the large recliner.

"You really look different, Qiana. I don't really know what it is." He stared for a moment and then sipped his hot tea.

"I'm pregnant," she said flatly. Russell gulped the tea and began to choke. She jumped up and handed him her napkin. He looked up at her as she cleaned the drips from the coffee table.

"Pregnant? What are you going to do?" he exclaimed.

"Nothing. I'm not going to do anything. I got pregnant on purpose." She smiled and went back to her seat.

"But Qiana, I mean. Don't you think I should have some say in this?"

"No, I don't. You see Russell, it's not yours," Qiana said calmly, though, she couldn't keep the smile from rising slightly to her lips.

"What do you mean, it's not mine?" he stood.

She suddenly grew afraid. It had been a long time since he had looked angry like this. He stood over her.

"So, you did it; you went out and got somebody else. I can't believe you," he said pulling her up from the chair. Her feet were barely on the floor now, as he gripped her arms tight.

She felt weak and instantly sick to her stomach. She had read about the nausea that would accompany pregnancy but this was different; this was the sick feeling that came with fear. She hadn't felt it in a long time but she recognized it immediately.

Russell let her go, after a long hard stare. Perhaps he was going to leave it at that.

She didn't feel the same aggression she had felt the day of the Superbowl, when she had been prepared to fight him back. Tonight she felt weak and helpless. She just wanted him to leave. She felt foolish for telling him about the baby. What was she thinking bringing him back into her world this way?

Suddenly, he grabbed the teacup and smashed it against her coffee table. When he turned back to her, it came with a backhand across her face. She stumbled backwards and fell. She screamed but her voice couldn't carry the pitch and volume she was trying to force upon it.

There was a knock on the door. It was Charles, she had told him to meet her here before they rode together over to their parents for dinner. She was going to tell them tonight about the baby. She had called Charles from work and told him to meet her at her apartment. She had planned on telling him first, and now he was at the door. She screamed out his name and the door burst open.

Russell stood his ground with fist still tightly clinched. Qiana held the chair as she helped herself to her feet.

"Russell." Charles' soft demeanor was straining, as he straightened his glasses. Qiana had never seen her brother angry. It just was not in his nature. Their parents were Christian people who had raised three soft and gentle souls, but tonight Charles was hard pressed to find an emotion other than the rage that was quickly building inside.

"Charles," Russell answered back, his nostrils flaring.

As the men stood, boring deep holes into each other's eyes, Qiana quickly grabbed her coat and purse.

"Get out Russell, I'm going to call the police, now just get out."

"We need to talk about this baby, Qiana," Russell said, through gritted teeth. Qiana's eyes flashed toward Charles, who only for a second took his eyes off Russell.

"And you hit her? She's pregnant and you hit her?" Charles said...before he went berserk.

It hadn't quite been the way she had intended for Charles to find out...but it was out now.

The police took Russell away after they spent almost an hour; it seemed, questioning the three of them.

It had been hard to convince them that Russell had been the instigator, when it was he who had sustained the most bruises.

"Girlfriend, Charles beat him so bad," Qiana told Rashawn over the phone, as she finished cleaning up from the evening's battle.

"Charles? Your soft spoken meek and mild mannered brother, Charles?"

"Yes, when he found out about the baby he flipped out."

"Speaking of baby...are you all right?'

"Oh yeah. I didn't fall hard or anything like that, I'm fine. But I know I have a bruise, it still hurts. I told Charles to tell mom and dad that I had to work late and would make it belated and then that would give me time to say that I fell or something creative like that."

"Think it will work?"

"No."

"So what are you gonna tell them?"

"I'll see what Charles told them first."

"Like I said, then what are *you* going to tell them?" Rashawn laughed, thinking about her own siblings' inability to keep her secrets from their parents.

"He said he wouldn't just go blurt out what happened, nor about the baby. But I know when they find out, however they find out, they are going to want a man. I need a man."

"Well, you've got a man."

"No I don't! There is no way I am going to tell them about, *that man*."

"Nigel Godwins," Rashawn said, with a lilt in her voice.

"Whatever."

"Say it…Nigel Godwins," Rashawn began to taunt.

"He's a jerk. I could tell that from the day at the clinic. I could tell that from the Superbowl party," she said.

"I thought he was cute. You said he was shy and…"

"On tape! I don't want to think about any of it right now. I just want to have my baby the way I planned."

"Do you want me to go with you go get the restraining order tomorrow? I don't go in until like one o'clock."

"No, my father is going with me. I know without even talking to him," Qiana said, giving in to the reality that Charles would indeed spill the beans about everything.

"Oh mannnn, your dad." Rashawn sounded like a teen caught out after curfew. "Well, you call me. And congratulations, girlfriend, on your baby," she said. "And your decision to keep it. I know that was a tough call. No baby or Nigel's baby…no baby or that fine man with those pretty eyes' baby," Rashawn continued to gibe. Qiana found herself giggling despite the sore jaw.

"Daddy, you didn't have to come with me. This wasn't hard to do," Qiana said to her father as they walked from the courthouse.

"Well, I wanted to talk to you," Andrew, Qiana's father, said in his soft voice, that all of his children had inherited.

He was a strong man, in good health, as he had been a physical education teacher since before Qiana was born. Even now, though he was reaching retirement age, he coached a city soccer team on the weekends. He had never fully approved of Qiana living with Russell and now she was going to hear about it. Just looking at the light discoloration on her face, that she had attempted to cover with make-up…just looking at it made his heartache and head hurt.

"Daddy, I'm thirty…"

"Thirty-six years old. I know, I was there," he smiled. "So that means I can't talk to you now? Thirty-five was that the cut off date? No more communication after thirty-five? Funny, Charles is almost thirty-seven and I can still talk to him."

"Talks too much," Qiana mumbled.

"What are you doing with your life?" Andrew asked, as they reached the car.

"Don't start. What do you want to know about my life?" she said putting her hand on her hip. She wasn't trying to be defiant, she was more nervous then anything.

"First of all, I would like to know who is this mystery man in your life? If you got a new boyfriend you could have just told us. We would have understood," Andrew spoke on, in his lecturing tone. Qiana looked off towards the sound of a motorcycle starting up. Charles had indeed told him about the baby. *She would have to remember not to speak to him, the next time they were together.*

She pondered her answer a long time. Just about then, she noticed Nigel Godwins strolling out of the courthouse. He wore a dark suit and carried a large briefcase. It was obvious he was working. His face was staunch and serious, and he looked much older than he had looked the last couple of times she had seen him. She spun around so that her back was to him. Her father noticed her movements and looked around.

"Are we dancing?" he asked. She fought to keep his eye contact.

"Ok, he's a nice guy. And I met him at uh…work. Yeah, he's a doctor…an OBGYN. Let's go now," she said and hurried him into the car. She would make up the rest while on the road.

As they drove from the parking lot they passed right by Nigel. He was getting into his car. He had donned his dark glasses. She irrationally worried that he would see her and stared straight ahead.

"It was too close a call for me," Qiana told Rashawn later on the phone.

"Then you should have just told your father the truth."

"I saw Nigel and just freaked out," Qiana admitted.

"Well, now you have to fix it."

"But you know something weird. I think one part of me wanted Nigel to see me…almost," she admitted in a half whisper.

CHAPTER 7

It was Monday and Monday's officially sucked. Actually, everyday sucked as far as Nigel was concerned. Everyday since the first of February, when he got the news from the *Family Makers* that his seed had been spread, life just plain ol' sucked.

The close brush with the gunman in the courthouse had faded and it was life as usual. He and Terrell hadn't even talked about it since giving the details to the police.

Nigel hadn't even told Sherry about Terrell saving his life that day. He knew it was just that he enjoyed having the knowledge deep inside, that Terrell was a better friend than Sherry could possibly understand…he was more like a brother.

"Nigel, you got a letter today from the *Family Makers*. What is this?" Sherry met him at the door holding his opened mail. His eyes widened as he snatched the letter from her hand.

"Don't you know it's a federal offense to open other people's mail?" He shoved the letter deep into his pocket.

"It was a request form…for you to rate their service. Why would you be on their mailing list?"

"Maybe a client…how in hell should I know," he snapped and walked past her.

"What is with the biting off of the head, Nigel? You know you have been doing this a lot lately," she glowered as she followed close behind him into the kitchen.

There were large pots sitting on the range and he thought that perhaps she had cooked dinner. He looked inside but as could be expected, they were empty. Sparkling clean as the day they were purchased.

"Why don't you ever cook anymore?" he continued on in his biting manner.

Reaching in the cabinet, he pulled down the Brandy and his favorite snifter and grabbed the remote, pointed it at the stereo. It was programmed to his favorite Jazz CD, which came on immediately.

"Maybe, because I don't think I like you anymore," she said as she put her hand on her hip and then grabbed the remote. She pointed it at the stereo, shutting it off. He downed his drink in one gulp and grimaced from the burn. It was good going down…took his mind off his problems for a second.

Bulk mailing from the Family Makers clinic, the thought made him mad all over again. He had decided not to pursue any legal action against the clinic. Especially since he knew Terrell would laugh him out of the conference room if he told his story about how everything had gone down…especially his…*not reading the contract,* part.

Having done the math, what were the odds anyway of some woman, actually getting pregnant with his donor specimen?

"Let's go to dinner," Sherry suggested, trying to ease the building tension.

"No. I've got a lot of work to do on this divorce I'm working on. I have to go up against Judge Montgomery soon. I had to have him served today. The man already hates me like…like…" Nigel tried to think of something really terrible to resemble what he felt Judge Montgomery's hatred for him could resemble, he couldn't. "Well anyways…he hates me more than anything. So, I know it's only going to get worse now that I'm representing his wife. He probably thinks I'm laying her too," he said, pouring another drink while he thought about her 'come-on' during their visit this afternoon.

"You remind me of my husband, Nigel. I don't know exactly what it is but you do," she said in that sultry voice of hers. She was hot for fifty-five. That face-lift had done wonders. "Not so much in your face but your overall build and mannerisms and well…" She touched his shoulder as she moved around behind him sliding her hands across the back of his neck. "I happen to find the Judge very attractive.

"Then why the divorce?" Nigel asked, as he nonchalantly removed her hands from him.

"There's just no fire anymore; no lust, no passion. When we got married thirty-six years ago there was a passion in that man. My daddy almost didn't want me to marry the cad…some of the things I had heard about him." She flung her hands and seemed almost to blush. "I didn't believe any of it. You know he wasn't very well off then. All of our money was mine when we first married. He worked in that pitiful little legal clinic in South San Francisco helping the poor and needy. He looked so funny," she said, giggling at the thought. "Those pale blue eyes and all that white hair. Even at twenty-five, his hair was white like that. Of course, he had more of it then." A derisive grin appeared, as a first rate fantasy now flattened.

"So you're wanting a divorce because you don't like him anymore?" Nigel scratched his head. She spun around to see his face.

"You know, you even sound like him now that I think about it. Maybe it's just me and I'm having some kind of pangs of conscious or something, but every time I'm with you, I leave wanting to call my husband and stop all this madness."

"I've never personally met your husband, I wouldn't know what he sounds like. But I'm sure it's just as you say, some pangs of conscious. Our minds can play tricks on us," Nigel sounded reflective as he thought about the recurring dream.

He had it just last night and he could still hear the music in his head but it wasn't clear enough for him to even hum the tune. In the dream he would know the name and every other detail about the song, but as soon as he woke up…it was gone.

He had talked to Terrell again about it but the best that he could suggest was they he needed to buy a boat, or go to a party.

"What about the black chick?" Nigel asked him, as they entered the elevator.

"I can't help you there…me and black chicks…ugh," he shuddered.

"You and Rita fightin' again?" Nigel asked. Terrell curled his lip.

"Marry me. Marry me," he said in mocking falsetto supposedly in imitation of Rita. "Don't women know any better lines to use after sex?"

"Like '*goodnight*' is a good one?" Nigel laughed as he stepped out onto the fourth floor.

"Works for me," Terrell said as the doors closed and he continued up.

Mrs. Montgomery had bothered Nigel that afternoon at the office and now the *Family Makers* had bothered him at home.

That night as Nigel lay in the big fluffy bed, staring at the ceiling, the full moon shown through the thin curtains. Sherry was still breathing heavily from their lovemaking. She moved close to him and rose up on her elbow.

"Nigel, what's wrong. Honey, no matter what it is, no matter how horrible, just tell me," she dramatized.

"Horrible?" Nigel chuckled as he smoothed her hair out of her face. She wasn't smiling now.

"It's nothing really, Sherry, but I do need to tell you something that I did," he began.

Sherry slid back into her gown and sat up in the bed to give him her full attention.

"I knew I wasn't nuts and something *is* going on," she said sounding anxious.

"No, nothing *is* going on, but remember way back when I told you that Dave wanted us to donate something like…like blood or something."

"You mean like back last year?" Sherry asked.

"Yeah, well, I didn't."

"What do you mean, you didn't?"

"I donated to the *Family Makers*."

"The *Family Makers*? Isn't that a sperm…"

"Yeah, a sperm bank. I didn't go through with the whole process. I did it-like, only a couple of times," he said. Sherry clicked on the lamp next to the bed on a small table. Her eyes were glazed now.

He had hoped for a glimmer of understanding but there was not even a trace.

"I don't believe you! How could you do that to me?" she shrieked and climbed out of the bed. She began waving her arms wildly, ranting and venting on about the last three years of her vital life.

"So much wasted time. So much wasted emotion," she continued as she pointed her finger at him. Nigel was beginning to fear she was going to lose all control.

"Sherry, could you calm down and listen to me," he began.

"And I was feeling terrible that I slept with James," she blurted.

Nigel was instantly floored. The words shot through his head like a spear, even she stood still for a second as if the words coming out had shocked even her.

"You slept with James?! The jerk from your office?" he exclaimed.

"He's not a jerk and yes! But only once, because I felt bad after!" she continued in her loud volume, not caring about the full impact of her confession.

"As opposed to feeling good after, where as you would still be sleeping with him," Nigel said, springing from the bed. Sherry stormed out of the bedroom; he followed.

"I don't believe you Nigel! I want a baby and you go and donate sperm. What's wrong with this picture?"

"While we are painting pictures, Sherry…" Nigel continued on, trying to keep the conversation on the track that lead to her explaining more about her affair with James.

"James wants a baby…Ohhh but not Nigel…he just donates sperm so that other women can get pregnant. But he doesn't want a baby," she continued on, not caring where the conversation was going.

"So are you telling me, you and this James character were trying to make a baby? And what, you were going to tell me it was mine? Well damn, Sherry, how was that supposed to work? Oh honey, remember that condom that broke? No? Oh sure you do," Nigel ranted on in his one sided conversation, as Sherry ignored him totally. "I would have never believed you. I have always been *way* to careful for that!"

"Oh sure, careful, you just have it directly inserted into strangers. I don't believe you expect me to understand what you did," she turned and growled. "I can't believe that you would rather impregnate a stranger than me. The woman you love!" she yelled at the top of her voice.

"The cheating woman!" he yelled back, matching her volume.

Taking her suitcase from the guestroom closet, she stormed back into the bedroom after stopping quickly by the bathroom and snatching her curling iron hanging there on the wall. She began to throw clothes in the suitcase. Nigel moved closer now, thinking he should maybe stop her.

Suddenly she switched on the cordless gadget and pointed it towards his exposed genitals.

"I wouldn't if I were you," she threatened.

Terrell met Nigel at the door. He looked deeply concerned and it showed on his face. Nigel almost felt bad that he had over reacted over the phone…but then again, had he? This was a disaster and it was one that had to be shared.

"Come in man." Terrell stepped back from the door and allowed Nigel to walk past. Rita was sitting on the sofa.

"I thought we could talk in private T. It's about that…you know, the thing I did," Nigel mumbled, avoiding eye contact with Rita. She was straining now to hear.

Terrell's face showed instant relief. He knew now, that no matter what Nigel had to say, if it was about the donation to the sperm bank, it could only be so devastating. What was the worse that could happen? Besides Terrell had already told Rita about that.

"Oh man, Rita knows about that? You told her about that?"

"Hey man, I tell my woman any and everything."

"Oh, you do huh?" Nigel said, showing mild irritation.

"Yes I do." Terrell's chest jutted out proudly.

"Well, did you tell your woman about when you and I went to Vegas instead of that conference, which really was not a conference at all? We just wanted to go to Vegas without your *Woman* along. Rita sat up straight on the sofa.

"What?" she asked.

"Nothing baby, nothing." Terrell fanned her on and then glared at Nigel.

"Oh, so then I guess there could have been no way he told you about the fifteen hundred dollars he lost at the crap table yelling, 'Who's your daddy?'" Nigel added in mocking imitation of Terrell at the crap table, blowing on the dice and shooting them. Rita jumped up from the sofa.

"I don't believe you clowns. You both are some lying clowns! I just thought it was you, Nigel. Giving your sperm out to strangers, who would do some crazy mess like that…but I guess it's even crazier to go to one of those places and buy some. I don't get that either," she said, thinking immediately of Qiana. "I don't get it at all. It's nasty to me." Rita started for the bedroom to give them some privacy, but before going inside, she swung around at Terrell, who had stood perfectly still, hoping she was going to let the revealing of his new found deviation from the truth stand unmentioned.

"And you, Mr. Liar, later for you," she said, slamming the bedroom door. Terrell sighed and took a deep breath. He then looked at Nigel with a frown.

"What's up with that man, divulging our guy thing?"

"Oh stop. She knows about the…the thing," Nigel said, sounding totally flabbergasted.

"Yeah man, you're right, I'm sorry. But she won't tell anyone. But what's up? I mean when you hadn't talked about it and I hadn't heard anything, I figured it was all worked out."

"Oh man, you won't believe the parade of errors this whole thing has been. I was just hoping it would go away or I would just wake up. The clinic; first I go back to get my stuff, right and then they say it's mostly gone, right? And then I was suppose to be a red cap but I'm a black cap or whatever crap they were saying. I'm thinking about suing 'em."

As Nigel continued to speak, he grew more and more animated, pacing the floor; venting and Terrell's face began to show more and more mortification with each new terrible development.

"They had me filed as a black man," Nigel sighed.

"So what are you saying?" Terrell finally asked as Nigel slumped down on the sofa rubbing his forehead.

"I'm saying, that for all I know, some black chick could be out there pregnant with my stuff, man."

"Some black chick is out there pregnant with your stuff," Terrell's words sounded heavy and full of doom.

The two men sat in silent thought.

"How could you have let something like this happen Nyge?" Terrell finally asked, as he stood and started for the kitchen. "You wanna beer?" he called back.

"Yeah why not."

"I mean, we need to celebrate you being a daddy and all," he chuckled wickedly. "Ya know I always wondered what it would be like if you were a black man. I mean, you are so close sometime, I forget you're not," Terrell said, handing him the beer. Nigel opened the Corona and chugged it.

"Yep, full blooded according to my mom." He ran his fingers through his light hair. "I don't get the light hair and eyes but my grandfather says it's from my father. He was from like some other part of Italy where they have blondes. I have never seen any blonde Italians in my family. I guess they exist but I've never seen one. Then he starts cryin' before I can ask anything more. I can't talk to him about my father. Come to think about it, I can't talk to neither him nor my mom about my father. It's almost like it's a big secret."

"Hey maybe..." Terrell sat forward on the sofa.

"Don't start, T. I had a father. A real guy. He just died that's all."

"So they tell ya. You need to find out more. I mean, you're gonna be a father now. You need to find out more about your father. He could have been like a circus midget or something."

"Terrell, we don't know that. I mean, about the pregnancy thing." Nigel chuckled at Terrell's comment about the possibility of him coming from carnival folk. "Do you know the odds of a woman getting pregnant with that little amount of sperm? That's like having sex like what...once? I mean the chances are like only one percent or something like that, really small. She is probably onto bigger and better by now."

"Well, I don't know about better...but definitely bigger," Terrell joked.

In the bedroom, against the door listening stood Rita, holding in all her emotions and any expression by holding her hand tight over her mouth.

It had been like pulling teeth to get Terrell to even tell her it had been Nigel that had donated the sperm. For weeks now he had just shook his head and said it was just one of the crazy white guys from work. But in the end it had been Nigel.

And now there had been a mix up. A mix up at the *Family Makers Sperm Bank,* the same sperm bank that Rashawn's friend, Qiana, had used. What were the odds of that? And Qiana getting pregnant on the first implantation…the first implantation made with Nigel's sperm…What were the odds of that?

"So what's up with Sherry?" Terrell finally asked as the men finished their third beers.

They were outside now shooting baskets in the neighbor's driveway. It was the only hoop on the street. It sat tall on its platform, at least ten feet high. It had four wheels but was un-moveable due the rocks and other heavy weights that lay on the base. It was open for all on that street to use. Usually the kids occupied it but today the kids were off doing other things.

"She's gone. She'll be back though…I know she will."

"Has she ever left you before?"

"Nope," Nigel said, and his seemingly easy shot, missed its mark by a mile. Terrell noticed and said nothing else about Sherry.

"Why don't you hang out here for dinner and stuff. I think Rashawn is cooking…maybe the two of you…" Terrell began, with light innuendo in his voice. Nigel chuckled as he felt a slight blush come to his face.

"You are always here now, don't you have a home?"

"Well hey, folks cook here. And I like to eat," Terrell joked.

Nigel knew why Terrell was always there. And he felt a little jealous. He knew he and Sherry had nowhere near what Terrell and Rita shared but still…he missed what they did have.

"Naw, I promised my mother and grandfather I'd have dinner with them tonight. Besides, I need to tell my mom, it's a big deal now. I've gotten myself in this biggo mess and don't even know how it happened. If nothing, else I need to tell her that Sherry left and then that will lead to why...and I could lie about that but it's just getting much too complicated. It's just my mom and my grandfather, I can tell them and just go home, right?" Nigel said not taking many breaths. Terrell stood staring at him, trying to decipher what he had just said.

"Sure," he finally said and then made his shot.

As Nigel drove into South San Francisco he rehearsed his lines. *How would he tell such an emotional woman that she would never see her first grandchild.* Nigel knew in her mind it would be as if it had been confirmed, no doubt about it...there was in fact a child on the way and it was purposely being denied to her. She wouldn't care about the odds leaning heavily towards the fact that nothing would come of this whole thing and that all of this would just turn out to be wasted emotion in the end. In her mind, Nigel's semen was out on the loose and surely some woman had conceived from it and now she would never see her grandchild...that was how she would see it. Why did he have to go through this with her? Why couldn't he just say he had made a mistake and he was sorry?

"It wasn't suppose to be a big deal," Nigel finally said out loud, as he slammed his fist against his steering wheel.

Perhaps he would just say nothing, change the subject, and get out of the evening just eating dinner and engaging in small talk.

There would be no chance of that, who was he fooling.

The light turned green and he turned onto the street to which his mother lived.

He loved that old street. It never changed.

Old families that had lived there for generations still had their homes there on that hill. Established foliage lined all the gates as he walked up towards her door, not like his neighborhood. Concrete walls and imported trees and shrubs were all that were there. Sherry had picked it out. It suited her. It reeked of money and those striving for money, everyone walking their fancy dogs and smiling those plastic smiles.

He hadn't given many thoughts to his goals lately, the goal to help his community, to give back. Now he understood what Dave wanted that morning when he asked everyone to donated to the big picture…to a life giving purpose.

As he looked around, the streets were filled with flowing sounds of music in the air, and laughter-children's laughter. He remembered now, the Marconi's had had another baby. He could swear he could hear the light voice of its crying off in the distance. He couldn't remember now whether it was a boy or a girl.

As he opened the gate to his mother's home, that he was proud to say he had paid off for her last year, he could smell the Pesto sauce. It was a special dinner. His heart sank. She had prepared his favorite meal and he was going in to break her heart.

"Nigel honey what's wrong?" she asked immediately after opening the door.

"Oh nothing ma. I uh had some beers earlier and I'm kinda tired now," he lied, avoiding her eyes by hanging up his jacket on the hook.

"Don't lie to me," she said flatly and walked back in to the kitchen. As he followed he began to smell that familiar odor of his grandfather's cigar.

"Oh wow, grandpa's here," he said as he rubbed his forehead and forced a smile.

"Where else would he be?" she asked sounding quite puzzled.

Dinner started out uncommonly quiet for the three of them, uncomfortably quiet. Finally Nigel's grandfather spoke up.

"So Nigel, how is the big world of law going?" He smiled and lit another cigar and pushed his plate away.

"Great Pop, it's just going great," he said, filling his mouth with more bread.

"And Sherry?" his mother chimed in.

"Great, she's going great too," he added, as his glance locked onto his grandfather's dark soul searching eyes. His stomach gripped. This was not good. Here he was a thirty-six year old attorney, scared to death of his mother and grandfather, afraid of what? Some deep old curse or malediction they could put on him? So he was lying and keeping secrets-so what? Like no one had never done this before to his or her parents.

He grandfather's eyes never moved from his.

"Ok ok, Sherry left me," Nigel finally blurted. "There are ya happy, I'm telling it," he said.

His mother hurried over to the table to look at him.

"Why? Why did she leave you? Were you unfaithful? Were you unfaithful like your…" She covered her mouth.

"What? What?" Nigel pleaded. "No, it wasn't that. No it was…unfaithful like my what?" Nigel asked noting his mother's abruptly shortened statement.

"Because if you were unfaithful Nigel, it's not your fault. Some men can't help themselves. Did you love her, this other woman?" His mother wrung her hands as she spoke full of emotion and sincerity.

"Ma, I wasn't unfaithful. We just couldn't agree on some things," he said trying to calm her down.

"What things?" his grandfather finally asked in a cold flat tone.

"Things," he said as he used his bread to sop of the remainder of his sauce from his plate.

"Was she unfaithful to you?" his grandfather continued in his questioning. Nigel tried to hide the wince that had instantly begun to tighten his eyes and cause them to burn.

"That bitch was unfaithful to you!" his mother yelled out. Her language took Nigel aback.

"No ma…it's not what you're thinking. She's not a bitch. Yes, Sherry cheated on me, but I drove her to it; I'm sure of it. She wanted to get married and have a family but I wasn't ready. I'm never gonna be ready for that."

Nigel stood still holding a crust of the hard-roll he was eating. He began to unravel his story as he marched around the table gesturing wildly with the bread still in his hand. He grew in emotion and frustration over the clinic's mix up with the specimen.

As he spoke he hardly noticed his mother's perplexed expression and his grandfather stillness.

"And that's the whole story," he finally exploded as he finished spilling his guts. There was silence and then only the sound of his mother stacking the empty plates from the table. She went quietly into the kitchen. Nigel wanted to follow her. He needed forgiveness, but instead he joined his grandfather at the table again.

"So, what sin do I qualify for, Pop?" Nigel asked looking down at his hands. His grandfather said nothing. Nigel then pulled the cork on the dark well-aged bottle of Merlot that sat on the small glass table under the window. He poured for his grandfather and they sat in silence while they drank.

"Nigel, why did you do it?" Nigel's grandfather finally asked.

"I just didn't want to donate blood. That's as deep as the thought went."

"Hmm." His grandfather re-lit his cigar. "I have a question," he began and left the words to hang in the air for a moment as if gathering his thoughts and savoring his smoke.

He wasn't that old, maybe seventy-five or so and the man was as sharp as a tack, Nigel thought to himself as he watched him. The smoke from his cigar floated around his head full of thick gray hair.

After Nigel's grandmother died everyone thought the man would fade away from sheer loneliness if nothing else, but instead he seemed to grow sharper and more alert each year. He was always up on current events and any other issue around him.

"So you donated your sperm to this 'bank' for some other women to get pregnant but you didn't want to be a father of a child you could see and be a part of his life," he said slowly. Nigel sighed. He hadn't made it sound any better than Sherry had.

"You make it sound so horrible too. I didn't want to be a father to anybody. The chances are one in a million any woman would even get pregnant," Nigel said loudly hoping his mother would hear. "I didn't leave that much," he whispered that part.

"I don't want to hear about your masturbation!" his mother yelled back. Nigel shook his head in frustration.

"Pop, it's not that big of a philosophical thing."

"But now Sherry feels as though you have been unfaithful to her?"

"Yes."

"And she has left you for another man."

"Yes."

"And you feel like you've done nothing wrong."

"Right. Well, until now," Nigel defended weakly as he glanced towards the kitchen where his mother was now ignoring him completely.

"Oh, don't worry about her, but tell me, what kind of a father do you think you would be?"

"A lousy father pop. I'm not ready. I don't even know what I would do if it came up and I don't want to find out! I'm not the hero my father was. The devoted man that he was, determined even to the death to be a good father. I've heard that story a million times," Nigel explained. His grandfather began to shake his head.

"Your father, your father, telling you that story…between you and me and the bedpost it was the wrongest thing she could have ever done, telling you that story. The next to the wrongest thing she could have done."

"What are you saying?"

"Don't start this," Nigel's mother said as she came from the kitchen. Her eyes were blazing in anger. Nigel had never seen that expression on her face before.

CHAPTER 8

The table was quiet as Qiana and her family sat together for their Easter dinner. Charles and his family were there, with little Jared in his Sunday best. Chalice and Marvin were there, looking loving as always. And Qiana was there alone, as had been the case for years now. Even while she was with Russell he would never join her for Easter dinner and once becoming Rufus, they never even expected him.

"It sure is quiet at this table," Chalice finally said. "So I guess I will start by saying, I am so cool and ok with this baby coming." She began buttering her bread roll. "I think it was a brave and decent thing for Qiana to do. I mean, if I didn't have Marvin and we weren't like, committed and together and in love…" She looked around, "I mean if I was alone like Qiana and getting old…"

Daphne, Qiana's mother cleared her throat. Chalice sipped her tea, pretending her taunting was unintentional.

"But who is the man, Qiana? We don't care that he's not your boyfriend or anything. I mean that's obvious because he's never around. And honey I don't want the details but we would just like to know," Daphne continued. "What's his name at least?"

All eyes were now on Qiana as she felt her seat grow hot and uncomfortable.

"I was artificially inseminated," she said finally.

There was a sharp silence and suddenly the table burst into laughter.

"No really," Qiana defended. The entire family, including Jared, was laughing now. Jared loved to laugh, even when he didn't get the joke. "Daddy, it's true," she pleaded, grabbing her father's arm as he wiped away the tears brought on by his hysterical laughter.

"Come on, girl, you know it's Rufus' baby. I didn't think so before. I actually thought you had got another man. But artificial insemination...paaleeeease," Charles chided. "Well, now, I'm really glad I kicked his loser butt."

"Only white people do stuff like that," Marvin added.

Everyone enjoyed his or her belly laughs and rude comments. No one seemed to notice that Qiana wasn't laughing, no one except Charles's wife, Selena. She was noticing Qiana's silent dignity as her family now made light of what was no doubt the biggest decision she had ever made.

"So did it hurt?" Selena asked as she and Qiana washed the dinner dishes, alone in the quiet kitchen.

"What? Them laughing? No," Qiana pouted.

"No, I mean the procedure. Did it hurt?" Selena asked. Qiana was taken aback for a moment and then smiled.

"No, not really. It wasn't any worse than anything else they do to us up in there," she giggled. Selena smiled and gave her a big hug.

"How did you know? I mean, why did you believe me?" she asked.

"Charles told me about what Russell did. I know if he were the father, he wouldn't have hit you. He just...I don't know...I just knew it wasn't his baby, not the way Charles said it went down that day."

"I thought he was going to kill me. I shouldn't have told him. He cheated on me, you know," Qiana added. Selena nodded showing that information too had made its way through the family grapevine.

"You sure are brave. I mean, you don't even know what your baby is going to look like. I mean, you can't even guess," she said setting the crystal in the cabinet.

"Selena," Qiana's voice lowered. "I do know. I found out who the donor was by accident."

"Oh my goodness, you're kidding."

"It's a lawyer. And he's not black," Qiana said. Selena's eyes widened.

"He was supposed to be black but they messed up at the clinic. It's a long story, but he's not black."

"Well, can't you like abort and start over or something or do you have to pay again? I mean you shouldn't it's not your fault," Selena asked in all sincerity. "Or does it even matter?"

"I thought I would care but after I went home and thought about my little Shorty. I just didn't care any more," she smiled. "Besides girl, he's fine," Qiana, giggled as she thought of Nigel's face. She hadn't wanted to admit it to herself how attractive she actually found him. She even found herself fantasizing that her baby would have his eyes…she loved Nigel's eyes.

"You've seen him?" Serena's voice got a little bit loud. Qiana closed the kitchen door.

"Seen him; I've spent time with him and everything. He is so different. I mean, he's like a jerk, but not."

"Well, does he know?"

"No, he doesn't know about me. I don't know if I should tell him."

"That might not be too good. You know lawyers, he might sue you or something."

"He can't sue me," Qiana chuckled. "He be my *baabee daadee*," she said giggling and then doing a little dance to the beat of the tune playing on the radio. Selena joined her.

Soon the two women had left off the dishes and were in full dance in the kitchen. It wasn't long before Charles joined them and they moved their dance to the dinning room. The stereo was cranked up and everyone began to enjoy the rest of the evening laughing, singing, dancing and happy.

Qiana thought more and more about Nigel as the days went on, thinking how maybe he should know about her baby.

"Or not," Rashawn said smacking her lips as she tried a sample color of lipstick at the cosmetic counter of Duncan's department store in the mall.

"But just think how you would feel if you had a baby walking around right under your nose. And what about when Shorty gets here and we are all together at your house for like Superbowl parties. Don't you think he is going to notice?" she added.

"You watch too many soaps. That man is not going to notice that nappy-headed baby is anything like him. Even when men know it's their babies they don't notice stuff like that," Rashawn said as they continued through the departments. "Let's go see the baby stuff upstairs," she suggested. Qiana hadn't thought much about what she would need.

"Well, I won't be shopping there. I'd be broke before he got two," Qiana sighed heavily after they left the pricey store and continued through the mall.

"What if…" Rashawn thought out loud.

"What if what?"

"Just say he did know and he liked the idea. What if he was giving you money to help out? How would you feel? I mean, what do you think?"

"I don't understand the question," Qiana said as she picked out two scoops of her favorite ice cream from among the flavors.

"What if he knew and decided that he would help you support the baby."

"You just said that wouldn't be a good idea. Make up your mind. Besides, didn't you hear him at that party? That man doesn't want no baby!"

"Maybe not with that woman. Did you hear her? I own this…I own that…she was a snob. Nigel seems like a sensitive man."

"Please. You almost made me cuss. You act like you know him. From what I saw he is just like Terrell, superficial and dumb," Qiana said deciding on some cookies too.

"Yeah, you're probably right but wouldn't it be cool if it just like, happened," Rashawn said looking dreamy eyed.

"Yeah right. I don't need him," Qiana said starting on the ice cream cone.

"I thought we were going to go eat some lunch?" Rashawn said noticing her snacks.

"We are," Qiana said sounding puzzled as to why Rashawn might be thinking differently.

Rashawn now gave more thought to the possibilities of Nigel and Qiana having a future together. What were the odds of it working out?

She discussed it with Rita.

"I don't know. Nigel is a strange bird. I mean, don't get me wrong. I really like him and Lord knows he is superfine for a Jew or whatever he is…but a father for Qiana's baby? I don't know. She is sorta naïve, don't cha think. I like her but I think that Nigel likes a tougher woman. Look at that white chick he was with, she was tough, man. Qiana is sort of soft, not a lot of toughness."

"She is just feminine. She has always been that way since I've known her. But when it comes to being like, straight up…you can count on my girl; she is there and gets the job done. I think Nigel should feel glad to have a woman like her be the mother of his child," Rashawn reasoned.

"But Shawn, Nigel works hard at having his own life and he has a life. Nothing like the life Qiana lives. Think about it; he lives in a biggo condo on the other side of town where the rich folks live. He drives that expensive car and wears those expensive suits…his shoes are like three hundred dollars a pair. He doesn't need some woman with a baby hangin' over his head. I mean look at his life; he goes to work and comes home and does what he wants. He golfs or whatever with his *pawdnas* on the weekend and can just get up and go when he wants. He can spend his money like he wants and nobody saying they need this or that. He's gotta give for love's sake not obligation."

"Are you talking about Terrell's life or Nigel's?" Rashawn asked. She noticed Rita's eyes widen.

"Maybe we could do something for her," Rita softened. "I mean, it's not like he has to marry her. At least he should know about the baby."

"Yep, the man needs to know where he's leaving his sperm around at," Rashawn snapped. Rita thought about it and then had to agree. Nigel should be responsible; after all, he was the father of Qiana's baby.

"So how is that supposed to work out?" Qiana asked the two sisters as they sat in her living room now, presenting their idea to her.

"You'll meet him; we'll set it up. And you'll hit it off and then you can tell him about the baby."

"I don't know if I want to do that. I'm not smooth like you guys are. I'm just frank. I'll blurt it out and say take it or leave it man," Qiana stated matter-of-factly as she finished her milkshake with a loud slurp. The girls looked at each other.

"Qiana, I think you are one of the most beautiful women I know. You're soft and sweet and except for you being so greedy these last couple of weeks..." Rashawn said, grabbing the big mug from Qiana's hands.

"I think that any man would be glad to have a baby with you. I mean if you had gotten black cap Mr. Stock Broker or whatever...he would have been missing out on ever meeting a wonderful woman. And Nigel, well, Nigel is lonely. He is all alone and needs somebody," Rita added.

"Yeah the white chick cut out on him as soon as she found out about you," Rashawn exaggerated. Qiana frowned.

"But I don't want him. And he doesn't want me," Qiana said as she opened her cookie and began to eat the cream center.

"But Qiana you don't understand, the baby will change all of that," Rashawn said.

"You guys talk about me and soap operas, Pa…leaz." Qiana got up and started for the kitchen for a glass of milk.

"You know if you get any more food I'm going to have to slap you," Rashawn called out.

"You try to set me and that white man up and I'm gonna have to slap you," she called back from the kitchen.

CHAPTER 9

Nigel saw himself now standing there at the foot of the Golden Gate Bridge, staring out over the vastness of the Pacific Ocean. The fog had lifted just enough for him to see the ship. It was more of yacht, a large white one. He could even see the Captain waving from the front window. He could hear the foghorn, summoning him down to the pier to meet for the party. But Nigel knew he couldn't meet them. He had an appointment and as he turned he saw her, a black beauty, tall and thin. Her eyes were dark and alluring, her gown flowed and clung tight to her flawless body as she approached him. She was saying his name but he was having to strain to hear it. He wanted so badly to hear her voice but he could not. As she reached him she outstretched her hand and he held it tightly in his. So small were her hands. And she was now not nearly as tall as she had been from a distance. He took her in his arms and they kissed. Suddenly there was music filling the air, it was the same song but this time he knew the band. It was the band, *Born Steady,* some of their older work, some of their more seductive music. He would have to remember that. He pulled her close as they moved together to the music. She was saying that she loved him in his ear and though he still couldn't hear her voice it made him smile. He knew later they would make love and he couldn't wait. He began to stroke her long neck and her smooth skin. He ran his hand down her waist when suddenly he felt it. He stepped back from the beauty only to see the round bulge under her clinging gown. She was pregnant. He backed away. His mind was scattering now as he could once again hear the yacht summoning him…honking for him…louder and louder. He had to go now. She called to him; her voice was heavy…almost manly…

"Nigel, come on man!" Terrell yelled louder towards the bedroom window and honked his car horn again.

Nigel sprung up in the bed. Looking at the clock as he gathered his thoughts, he realized he was in a sweat. It was Saturday, eight a.m. He was to hit the golf course with Terrell and Smithy.

"You've been quiet all morning, feeling alright?" Terrell asked finally as they strolled toward the seventh hole. Smithy had lagged just a little behind giving them a minute to have a private word.

"Nothing, just a rough night," Nigel admitted. "I keep having that dream. It's more like a vision really," he said.

Terrell positioned his club, "You told me about that…still having it, eh?"

"Am I to understand that you are having a reoccurring dream? I'm pretty good at figuring those out," Smithy chimed in.

"You can't even pass the bar. You aren't good at figuring anything out," Terrell teased as he took his swing.

"Oh go on with ya." Smithy chuckled in his usual lighthearted manner.

"It's this beautiful black chick, I mean fine as wine, man. And it's that old group, I can't think of their name. I can never remember when I wake up, but I'd know if I heard it again, anyways, it's playing in the background." Nigel began to explain to Smithy for the first time.

"Always the same song?" Smithy asked as he took his stroke.

It was Nigel's turn now.

"Yeah, and there's this yacht, I haven't figured out if the yacht is mine or not or even if it's important but it's always there. Anyways, we're just about to get it on and boom…there it is." Nigel swung hitting the ball further than he had all day. "She's pregnant," he said without looking at the either man. Terrell and Smithy watched the ball sail through the sky.

The three men paused there looking up at the sky before finally Smithy spoke, "Do you know the woman?" he asked in his usual sincere, almost perky tone. "Do you think she might have some significance to the dream? Maybe you are growing more attracted to black women and you don't want to admit it," he added.

"Nigel doesn't have a problem with black women. You don't get it Smithy; you weren't there since the beginning of this dream thing, so don't try to figure it out. I told you, you were no good at this," Terrell explained. "I already told him what the dream meant. It means if he takes a boat trip, he's gonna die."

Smithy pondered if he should say anything else helpful and then changed his mind as they continued on to the next hole.

"Hey why not we go out tonight? Rita's been bugging me to go out. My schedule is light next week. I'm not working on any closings or anything so I told her yeah. I think her sister is going with us and maybe that friend of hers," Terrell offered.

"And maybe the friend is black and beautiful and you'll be able to resolve some of your conflicts over black woman and your resistance to wanting to pursue a relationship. Or maybe it's the band, maybe that's where the conflict lies and it's not the black chick at all," Smithy mumbled as he walked slightly ahead of Nigel and Terrell.

"But can you tell me if the boat is mine?" Nigel asked as he trailed behind. "It's a really nice boat."

"I can't help you with the boat Nyge," Smithy answered.

The club was full of smoke or fog, one or the other; Nigel couldn't tell. He just knew he hadn't been to a real dancing club in ages and this was very reminiscent of many of clubs that he would leave with his head bad, and totally hung over from in the morning.

He figured it must have been one of Rita's strange moods that had gotten them all here. She was forced to wear business suits and carry on conversations with confused teens all week and perhaps, letting her hair down was what she looked forward to…all Nigel knew was she was one

woman who had it down to a science. As he approached the table he
smiled at Rashawn. She was looking very *hot* tonight and for a second
he found himself staring.

"They are out there dancing." Rashawn pointed toward the dance
floor and spoke loudly to get above the music. Nigel tried to see them
through the dancing lights and many bodies, but it was impossible. The
waitress met him before he had a chance to even sit.

"Bourbon straight up," he said close to her ear. She smiled at him and
walked away. He sat down. At that moment he noticed the round-faced
girl from the Superbowl party coming through the front door. He
started to motion for Rashawn to turn but was immediately stunned
when she removed her jacket. She was draped in a soft flowing white
dress, much like the one the woman in the dream wore. He closed his
eyes tight and then opened them again. As she approached the table her
long braids draped her face. She looked angelic, almost like a painting...the Mona Lisa to be sure.

Nigel stood to offer his seat. She smiled at him and took the seat next
to Rashawn, who noticed Nigel's reaction to her immediately.

"I can't believe you came. I didn't think you would," Rashawn spoke
loudly to the girl and smiled broadly. She just nodded. "This is Nigel,"
Rashawn introduced. She nodded again.

"I think we've met," she said, her normally soft voice straining to get
above the music. Nigel couldn't really hear her and he found himself
now in an awkward moment of deja vu.

"Your name, I can't remember your name," he said to her. The waitress reappeared. She asked Qiana what she wanted to drink. She shook
her head. But the waitress insisted that a minimum of at least one drink
would have to be ordered according to policy.

"Virgin Colada then," she ordered.

She started to open her small purse to pay when she caught Nigel's
eye. He smiled, as he had already paid the waitress for both drinks and
tipped her.

It was retro night and as the DJ ended a remix of the *Gap Band's, Party Train* and as luck would have it a slow sensuous older song by the *Isley Brothers* began to play. It wasn't the tune from the dream but Nigel felt compelled to ask her to dance anyway.

"Would you like to dance?" He reached out for her hand. She accepted. Rashawn was stunned at what was happening right in front of her. This was going to be easier than if planned. Qiana had refused to set Nigel up but here it was happening anyway. He liked her immediately…Rashawn could tell.

On the dance floor her small hands filled Nigel's easily as he pulled her in close. The flashing colored lights changed to a blue haze that covered them. He began to feel as if they were alone out there on the floor…holding her…closer and closer. She whispered something in his ear. He leaned in close to hear. She smelled fresh like…like peaches. That wasn't in the dream either, but he liked it.

"My name is Qiana. I don't think I got to tell you earlier," she smiled.

They stared deep into each other's eyes. She wasn't as tall as the woman in the dream was but surely she was as beautiful. Maybe it was her make-up, but she looked more glamorous tonight than the day of the Superbowl. Nigel found himself about to kiss her. He couldn't believe it. What was he thinking? He stepped back from her.

Just at that moment Terrell and Rita bumped into them and Nigel noticed the music had changed to the livelier beat of *Lakeside*. They didn't leave the dance floor, but continued to dance for what seemed to be hours.

Qiana was surprised at how good a dancer Nigel was. He hadn't mentioned that on his cassette either…he should have.

Later, the group, Terrell and Rita, Rashawn and the nice guy from the table by the door, Qiana and Nigel all left for the Peppertree restaurant, nearby.

The table conversation hit on many topics from politics and law to the lighter side of people and their issues.

"Ok, I need to have a better reason why we are not married Terrell," Rita said in retort to something mentioned that started the whole marriage conversation.

"Because, married people fight too much and…and…and…" he stammered. "When people are married they start taking liberties with each other," Terrell said trying to regain confidence. "I'm a lawyer, I know how it works. Verbal contracts are broken all over the place and who you gonna sue?" he added. The nearly inebriated nice guy from the table by the door raised his glass in a toast to agree.

"I was married once," he added. "I even have three kids and now I don't even get to see them."

"Yes! Marriage makes single parents too," Terrell added. Rita slapped his arm and nudged her head towards Qiana. Terrell mistook her nod to be towards Nigel.

"Nigel isn't a single parent…not really. I mean he *makes* single parents but he isn't one," Terrell said. Nigel raised his hand in denial.

"Now, we can't assume that! Who ever she is…she could be a perfectly happily married woman," he said chuckling.

It was getting easier to joke about the whole thing now. With Sherry gone and the specimen gone…what else could he do but laugh. Terrell was always good at helping him see the lighter side of everything.

"She was talking about me, T. I'm going to be a single parent…by choice, thank you," Qiana spoke up finally.

"Oh my Gawd there is a pregnant woman in our midst!" the nice guy from the table by the door chuckled, unaware that Nigel's eyes had grown as wide as two baseballs.

"You're pregnant?" he gasped as his stomach instantly reacted to the news.

"Yes I am," Qiana admitted. Rashawn squealed at the realization that this would be the night they hadn't planned, but hoped would happen. Qiana was going to do it; she was going to tell him.

"You didn't tell me," Terrell said to Rita.

"I was sort of trying to keep my news to myself but since it's come up. I'm pregnant. I even know the exact day I got pregnant."

"Boy you're pretty sure about yourself. Whose the lucky guy?" Terrell asked. Rashawn nudged him again.

"What? What's with the nudging here? Qiana is pregnant and I just was axin who knocked her up?" he queried. The table grew suddenly very quiet.

"Well, I can see here that I'm in the middle of an insider's story." The guy stood. "Perhaps I should leave," he said without being noticed. "Rashawn? I'll call?" he added. She nodded without looking at him, as she was totally engrossed now at the drama unfolding here at the table. "Ok, I'll do that," he smirked and walked away.

"The father of my baby is a really nice guy," Qiana said. "I mean he has a really nice sense of humor and I think I like him."

"You *think* you like him? You say it like it was a business deal. Like you chose him out of the crowd," Nigel said, sounding almost miffed. Qiana's eyes began to bore a hole in him. The chemistry they had shared since the beginning of the evening was now, somehow, turning into a bad experiment.

"I wouldn't say a crowd," Qiana defended.

"What's up with you women acting like men are just baby-making factories; just waiting for ya'll's temperatures to be right!" Nigel vented, mentally finishing up his argument long past and lost with Sherry.

Qiana now wanted another day...another way to tell him, not tonight, nor this way...not in front of everyone like this.

It wasn't like she was thrilled that the clinic had made the error and she was not going to be giving birth to the proud African Prince the way she had always fantasized her son to be. It wasn't her fault that the town of so small that it brought the world just a little closer around them to where things like this could really truly happen. It wasn't her fault he was a jerk.

She knew if the truth began coming out it wasn't going to come out right at all. Nigel was ticking her off. Perhaps it was the way he was glaring at her with those glass-like eyes of his. Perhaps it was that little bit of an attitude coming up in his tone, as if he knew her well enough to have an attitude with her.

'How dare he', she began to think.

"Nigel, you know what?" Qiana said as she felt her pointed index finger, rising towards his face.

Rashawn knew suddenly that the moment she had hoped this was turning into was fading quickly into something bad.

"What?" Nigel challenged, ignoring her confrontational position.

They all sat quiet as Nigel and Qiana glared with instant rancor towards each other, neither knowing exactly where the feelings were coming from, but neither being able to stop them from coming.

"Nothing." Qiana slid from the booth. "Nothing at all," she sighed and opened her purse, laying out her money for her share of the tab. She turned and with head held high, marched out. "What a nightmare," she could be heard saying as she left.

Rashawn and Rita looked at each and sighed heavily.

"What the hell is going on?" Terrell exploded in a total state of confusion. "What was that?" He pointed towards the direction of Qiana's exit from the table.

"Qiana is pregnant," Rita said under her breath.

"Yeah, I got that much." Terrell sat up giving his full attention to Rita who was now looking rather sheepish as she began to nibble her potato skins. Terrell pulled her fork from her lips.

"What's up?" Terrell asked again. "Why did she have an attitude towards my man Nigel here?"

"Qiana went to the *Family Maker's* to make a baby ok…so when she got there, her friend…I won't mention her name…gave her a profile and a cassette. She told her that because she knew her, she would her start with a virgin…you know, being cute. Qiana fell for voice on the cassette and bought the sperm number that went with the cassette…or so she thought. The new girl that didn't know what she was doin'…thought she did, but she didn't…she had already messed up everything. Nigel was suppose to get a red cap and he got a black cap put on his sperm. You know black for black, white for white and red for…well…Nigel. What you are anyways, Jewish?" Rita took a deep breath as she noticed all eyes were on her. "How did I get picked to tell the story anyway?" she squirmed.

"What are you saying?" Nigel said staring deep into Rita's large dark eyes, which were now darting towards her sister.

"Now Nigel, she wasn't sure until the day you came back to get them. She heard you say seven fifty and then she knew," Rashawn piped up. "All we could do was hope that she wasn't pregnant but…" She forced a sheepish smile to her face. "She didn't want you to know…honestly."

There was now only a deafening silence that covered the table.

"This is incredible. This is…incredible. I don't believe it…it's so incredible." Nigel stood from the table. He was angry and he couldn't even attempt to hide it now. His thoughts scattered as he tried to think back on all he had just said to Qiana. It was too late now to even try to think of what he might have said differently, had he known.

He took a twenty from his wallet to cover his late night snack and threw it on the table. He patted his pockets for keys and without looking at anyone sitting there, started for the door. "Damn incredible," he could be heard saying as he walked out of the restaurant.

"Well, I'd say this went well," Rashawn said putting her hands deep into her lap. Rita didn't look up at anyone but continued to nibble her appetizer.

"I think it went very well," she added.

"I think all you people need to be taken out and shot," Terrell said as he finished his ice tea and called for the tab.

CHAPTER 10

Nigel had avoided Terrell all week. He wasn't angry with him...not really. He wasn't angry with anyone, he just needed to sort this whole thing out and he knew Terrell would be of no help at all...he just knew that. It was hard enough for him to believe that this whole thing was happening.

He knew Rita and Rashawn had no reason to lie to him about Qiana; of what benefit would that have served any of them, especially Qiana? It was obvious she wasn't thrilled about the whole thing...'*What a nightmare*', she had said, and Nigel heard her loud and clear.

The longer Nigel pondered the situation actually, the better it was getting. At least now he knew where his specimen had gone. It was remarkable and a miracle to be true, but no longer a mystery.

He had it all figured out, he would simply pay whatever fees Qiana had incurred, perhaps a little more for emotional damages after the abortion she would have; he would pay for that as well. Surely she would understand why she had to get one. She seemed like a reasonable woman, very calm in her nature and actually quite easy to talk to, soft even. It would be a piece of cake.

He had spent the week calling around for prices of abortion clinics and procedural information. It all sounded so gruesome but...hey...women did it all the time.

As he paced his living room, which had become his habit, the phone rang.

It was Sherry.

"Oh my, Sherry." Nigel grinned, as he looked around self conscious now of all the notes about clinics and other incriminating paraphernalia. He began to gather it all up as he spoke.

"Were you busy, I mean, I know you weren't expecting me to call you."

"No! No, I'm not busy."

"The more I thought about why we broke up the more I realize that I over reacted."

"Over reacted?"

"Yes, I see now that I might have. I did some research and it said that only like point two percent of every woman inseminated ever even get pregnant." She had a smile in her voice. Nigel sat forward.

"Yes, and the odds of anyone choosing my…uh…number, well that lowers it still." He closed his eyes tight hoping to ease the pain gripping his stomach.

"Can I come over?" she asked flatly.

"Yes! I mean…sure you can," he chuckled nervously. It had been over a month since he had seen her. He was surprised how much he in fact did miss her.

She rang the bell, as she no longer had a key. Nigel gave the living room one more look around for neatness. He had spent the majority of the hour cleaning the bedroom. He had grand hopes of ending up in there.

He opened the door and she walked in. She had roses. She often would bring him a rose after a small fight so the fact that she had a dozen showed Nigel this one had indeed been a biggy. Her dress was red, tight and short and her heels were high. Nigel could recognize freshly painted toenails a mile away. He wanted to touch her body beyond her shoulders as he took her flowers and removed her trench coat.

"Let me put them in some water," she smiled, taking the roses from him and disappearing into the kitchen.

"So, how is James?" Nigel couldn't resist asking. He heard nothing from the kitchen. She reappeared carrying two wineglasses.

"I noticed the wine airing so I thought I'd just pour us some." She handed him his glass. "Did you ask me something while I was in there?" she asked her voice high pitched and fake.

"No, it wasn't important," he said and then kissed her. She threw her arms around his neck spilling her wine on the carpet. Nigel, taken aback at her aggressiveness, sat his glass on the dining room table and then took her glass from her. They both giggled as she began to undress him right there in the living room. Never before had Nigel's mind soared with confusion like this, where Sherry was concerned. He was unzipping her dress before he could think of any questions to ask as to why she was so filled with lust and want of him. As soon as they both were naked she pulled him down to the floor on her.

"Sherry wait, you know the condoms are in the bedroom."

"Damn the condoms, Nigel," she moaned and pleaded.

"No, Sherry, no damning the condoms," Nigel said as he rose to his knees. Her face grew red with either embarrassment or anger; at that moment Nigel wasn't sure which. He stood and reached for her hand. "Let's go in the bedroom, baby," he spoke softly. She didn't move. Her blue eye cutting through him was all he could feel now. "Ok, let me go in there and get them. I say *them* because you seem rather amorous tonight," he joked, using an exaggerated French accent, hoping to ease the ever-building tension.

Suddenly she was on her feet. Taking her coat out of the closet and putting it on without dressing, she grabbed up her dress and under things and threw them over her arm.

"Sherry, what was this all about?"

"I try to make up with you and you…you." She fought to hold back her tears. Nigel grabbed her by her shoulders and looked deep into her eyes.

"You weren't trying to make up with me here. What is going on?"

"James is sterile," she said slightly above a whisper. Nigel rubbed his head and then grabbed his pants.

"Ahh," he said as he jumped around on one leg until he caught his balance enough to put them on. He wanted to appear smoother and more sophisticated at this moment but it was impossible. He was flustered and irritated. "So I was like…uh…donating again huh?" he smirked and gulped his wine.

"Anyway, I need to go, Nigel," she said flatly.

"Oh, now you're just gonna leave. Just like that? No wine…no…no sex…oh yeah I forgot, I'm only in it for love making, Sherry…not for baby making!" He was raising his voice now.

"Keep your voice down," she said as she opened the front door.

"My voice? You're the one running into the street naked, Sherry!" he continued his diatribe. She slammed the door and spun around facing him.

"Fine, Nigel, let's go jump in the sack! Let's get your condoms and your precautions," she screamed as she threw down her clothes. Hot tears were streaming down her face.

"All I want is a baby. Is that so hard for you to understand?"

"Why is this turning into a melodrama? I don't get it. First Qiana tries to trap me now you try to trap me. I don't want a baby! Not yours-not Qiana's!" he vented on. Sherry closed her eyes tight and then let the confusion come to her face.

"Who is Qiana?"

"You've met her," Nigel said and began to laugh maniacally. "I've met her. We're all friends!" He stomped into the kitchen and began to pour wine into a glass and then, changing his mind; he decided to drink from the bottle. "Confidentiality? I'm a lawyer for Christ's sake.

I'm not supposed to be dealing with things like this. I need to sue somebody. They think just because she's nice and all, that I'm ok with this. I'm not ok with this." He turned to see Sherry standing in the kitchen. Her coat had opened and Nigel couldn't help getting one more longing look at her body before storming past her.

"What are you talking about? Who's pregnant?" Sherry asked as she followed him. He could hear the click of her high heels against the hardwood as she hurried to get in front of him. He turned up the bottle once more to his lips.

"Qiana, the cute little black chick from the Superbowl party," Nigel said in a calmer voice now.

"You got the cute little black chick from the Superbowl party pregnant; the nurse? I remember her now, the nurse. I can't believe that Nigel."

"I didn't get her pregnant; not directly anyway. I guess you could call her one in a million." He flopped onto the sofa. Sherry came and sat next to him. They sat quiet for a moment and then Sherry smiled.

"We are a mess, Nyge," she said adapting Terrell's nickname for him. "Here I am, wanting a baby and ending up with James, sterile as a rock and you don't want a baby and you have one on the way…with a stranger."

"Are you happy?" he asked, patting her hands. She nodded.

"I thought I wasn't, but I am. We have a lot in common ya know. We went to Utah and guess what, our folks even live near each other. Small world huh?" she giggled. Nigel's head spun from the wine.

"Too small," he said trying to force a smile.

"Well, you have to tell me how you found out it was *that* girl," she said and then shook her head. "I'm sorry; God, I'm just so jealous I can barely breathe; *Qiana*, how did you find out Qiana was carrying your baby?" She tried to force a caring tone onto her words.

"Quite by accident really," Nigel began telling her the events as best be could through combining Lorraine's explanation of events at the clinic and Rita's fast told story at the club that night. "I'm going to offer her a lot of money to get an abortion," he finished speaking.

Suddenly he was beginning to feel badly about how cold and unfeeling he sounded. Sherry hadn't said much while he explained the situation. After he finished she stood and took his hand and pulled him up from the sofa.

"Well, it'll all be over soon and you can get your life back," she smiled, satisfied at how it was all going to come out. "I mean, maybe this was meant to be, you and I splitting up like this."

"Yeah, maybe. I'm really sorry I couldn't give you what you wanted. I guess I even sorrier that James can't either," Nigel said feeling truly sincere.

"One more time for old time sake, Nigel? You look like you could use it." She smiled and nodded towards the bedroom. "Safe and sound as always," she whispered in his ear.

After she drove away Nigel stood in the doorway a long time looking out, unable to sort his feelings. This was the closest he had ever felt with Sherry. It was like for a moment they were friends and she understood what he was feeling.

She was never going to come back; he knew that for sure now. He pulled a rose out of the vase and inhaled it aromatic scent; it was very calming.

He needed to see his grandfather.

He was about to make some big choices in his life and he was going to need some help.

CHAPTER 11

Nigel drove slowly through the parking lot until he reached the 'staff' parking. He knew that little red sports car anywhere; she was here. He parked and strolled casually onto the campus. He went into the administrative office in hopes of getting some clue on where to find Rashawn. He had waited a couple of weeks until he had all his facts together…he had prepared his case and was ready to present it to Qiana.

Now he needed Rashawn…

"May I help you?" the young, casually dressed girl, at the reception counter asked Nigel.

"Sure, I'm looking for Rashawn Maxwell."

"Oh Dr. Maxwell? She is so cool, she is in class right now though." A grin crept onto the girl's face. Nigel wondered why everyone in college always appeared to be stoned? Why did their conversations always seem to go *lateral* to the actual conversations taking place?

"And that class would be?" Nigel asked.

"Ethics, but it's too late to add ya know," she added.

"No problem. Do you think you could give me an idea of where that class is?" he asked. He was trying not to think too very hard on the fact that Rashawn was teaching a subject that seemed so out of everyone's scope at the moment.

"Over in the lecture hall." She pointed vaguely in a northerly direction. Nigel immediately grew frustrated and put on his sunglasses to hide his eyes. He was sure he was glaring at her.

"Thanks," was all he could say as he left the building.

The campus was larger than he had ever remembered it being when he had dated a girl that went there…years ago. Finally he sat down outside the cafeteria to wait, hoping that perhaps she would pass and sure enough, there she was. There was no mistaking her sexy saunter, as she approached the cafeteria. Even in a business suit and at a distance, Nigel felt Rashawn had an air about her that said, '*I am all woman, look at me*'.

She hadn't noticed him until she had nearly passed him and was startled when he called out to her.

"Oh my Gawd," she giggled, nervously looking around. "What are you doing here?" she finally asked.

"Qiana's address…I need it," he said flatly. Rashawn's smile left her pretty face.

"For what?"

She continued walking into the cafeteria. He strolled with her.

"Qiana and I have a situation and we have to get it resolved," he said in his usual casual manner. Rashawn greeted a couple of her co-workers with smiles and small talk as Nigel waited patiently.

"Rashawn, look I don't have all day," he finally said as she purchased her sandwich, seemingly ignoring his growing impatience for the last ten minutes.

"Nigel, why would I help you hurt my best friend? Why would I do that?" she said in a tone she had never taken with him before.

He had never seen Rashawn in her work environment and he had to admit she was almost intimidating with her dark suit and staunch manners.

"Because, I want to help her," Nigel said.

"Help her what? Help her raise her baby? She doesn't want nor need you to do that. Qiana is totally happy to have this baby alone. She doesn't need you or your money or your patronizing. I know her, you don't know her," Rashawn continued, in a cool tone.

Her dark eyes were like pools of hot lava, burning a hole in him. "She is not going to just sit back and let you waltz your little butt into her life and change her plans. Ok, so we were wrong, we thought you should know; sue us," she giggled sarcastically.

"Come on Shawn, you have to see how bad this is? Ethically speaking," he said sounding totally tongue in cheek now.

"Bad for whom? You seem like a man scared of something, Nyge. There's no big bad monster out there. It's just a little bitty baby. Or is it Qiana you're afraid of...*Ethnically* speaking?" she said slyly and then winked at him. Nigel looked away from her. This conversation was beginning to bother him. "I saw you. You like her. At least you did until you found out you got her pregnant."

"I didn't get her pregnant," Nigel snipped. "Not directly...and you are so way off," he smirked.

"I can't give you her address because you can't promise me that you won't go over there pushing your views around?" she argued as she took a large bite from her sandwich.

"I have to say what I feel," he admitted.

"Why? Why do men always have to say what they feel?" She rolled her eyes.

"Oh give me a break." Nigel literally swayed from her comment.

Rashawn finally let out a chuckle and underneath all of her hard front he began to see the woman he knew, the playful one that would give in to him with just a little more pressure and a bit of boyish charm. "Ok, I promise I won't upset her," he said, knowing it was only a half-truth he spoke. He knew what he would say may upset her...at least in the beginning, but surely in the end she would have to see things his way and come over to his way of thinking. It was a simple clear proposition he had to offer her. What other way was there to see things?

"Please?" and that was the best he could do, for a closing argument, but he had a strong feeling it was going to work.

The next morning, Qiana's mother had showed up early to spend the day with her. Qiana had gotten prepared for the visit and possible invasion into her personal life…and was actually looking for to it. She had many questions about the baby and motherhood to ask.

She could swear she was showing even though no one seemed to notice but her.

"Qiana, you are not showing. You are getting fat but you are not showing," her mother insisted as she helped her fold clean towels that bright Saturday morning. "How many months are you now?"

"I'm almost four months. Doctor Steward said I am coming along great and it looks good. I don't have to check in with the doctor at the *Family Makers* anymore, I start seeing my regular OB, Doctor Young, next week."

"*Family Makers*…that sperm bank downtown? Qiana, don't start that crazy talk again about that artificial stuff," her mother giggled. "You made us laugh like crazy that night. You can be so funny sometimes," she said starting for the hall closet that held the linen.

Just about then, Daphne paused at the window that faced the street. She noticed a handsome medium built man, dressed in a business suit, standing at the curb looking toward her apartment. He was looking at a notepad and glancing up toward the window.

"Qiana, do you know him?" she said, pointing out the window. Qiana looked out only to see Nigel coming up the walk.

"Oh no," she gasped and dropped the blinds quickly.

Rashawn had called and said that Nigel may show up, as he had cornered her at work the day before, and *forced* the address out of her.

There was a knock on the door.

"Mom don't get that," she snapped. Daphne stood still, in a quandary over at what to do next.

"Qiana," Nigel could be heard calling through the door. He had seen the blinds close he knew she was home.

Her stomach tightened at the sound of his voice.

"Qiana, who is that?" her mother asked.

"Nobody," she answered quickly.

"Oh my goodness, is this why you told us that story? Is he the father? Is that white man the father, Qiana?" her mother insisted.

"Yes mama, but it's not like you think. I did go to the *Family Makers*. You just have to understand, I didn't mean for this to go this way. It was all supposed to be confidential."

"Qiana, we really need to talk," Nigel continued, through the door. "I am prepared to make you an offer and I think you should hear it."

She opened the door slowly. He took a step forward but saw she wasn't going to budge the door any further.

"I would like to talk to you about this situation we seem to have found ourselves in."

"Situation? I don't have a situation," she said. Her mother hunched her hard.

"Let that man inside. Don't talk your private business at the door," she whispered.

"We don't have any private business."

"Qiana, I would like to offer to pay for you to have an abortion," Nigel said, sounding flat.

Qiana's heart sank as she heard her mother gasp from behind her. She would have to explain everything now...again.

"Go away Nigel. I paid to have this baby, it's mine and I have a right to have it," she said coldly.

"That's what I'm saying. I will reimburse your fees so you can start over and pay for the abortion and whatever else you think would be fair. I have drawn up a contract," he began. Qiana thought about what he was saying to her for a moment. What could she say?

Suddenly before she could think, her mother opened the door full swing.

"You need to hit the road Mr.! She's already had about all the help she could need from you, no return, no refund!" she said and slammed the door as hard as she could.

"Oh my, I really lost it," Daphne said in her normal soft voice as she attempted to regain her composure. Qiana giggled at her mother's attempt at getting *really* angry.

Nigel stood stunned for a moment and then returned to his car. So much for Qiana being a cream puff, he thought to himself. He ripped the page that had her address on it from his notepad, crumpled it and threw it in the street. 'So much for it being a piece of cake,' he cursed under his breath as he looked back towards the apartment only to see Qiana peeking from behind the blinds.

"Pop, what did I do wrong?" he asked. "I was honest, and straight forward and I think pretty damned generous." He now regretted he hadn't come to his grandfather first, before going over Qiana's house.

Nigel sighed as the two of them strolled through the park. Children played all around him.

He picked up a ball that had rolled astray and tossed it back to some small children playing kickball.

"Nigel, you need to think deep on what you did today."

"I did. I thought very deep. I don't want a baby and I don't want my child being on this planet unwanted."

"But you got her pregnant."

"I did not. Not directly, I mean…it was my…stuff; I made sure of that when I went back to the clinic again, but I did not get her pregnant."

"But you knew some woman somewhere would get pregnant," he reasoned. Nigel didn't like where this conversation was going.

"But I wasn't suppose to find out."

"So that means you didn't do it, because you didn't know?" he smiled slyly. Nigel felt embarrassment cover his face.

The two men walked quietly along for a few moments before Nigel's grandfather spoke again,

"But she is wanting a baby. And from what you say to me, it's not your baby she is wanting, anyways. So seems to me she is stuck as well," he chuckled and puffed his cigar. He rattled out the quirky Italian phrase that Nigel had learned when very young that basically said…

'The price paid for arrogance is never cheap'.

"Do you like her?" he asked in English.

"That doesn't matter," Nigel answered quickly wanting very much to avoid that part of the conversation. "Pop, I want to want my children. I want to feel like ma and my father did when I was born. I mean, I can just tell I was like…wanted, and I want my…"

"Hold on a minute Sonny, you weren't as wanted as you think. It's the time you know the truth. I have gotten almost sick at my stomach hearing this about your 'so-called' father; sick I tell you," he spat. Nigel was shocked at his grandfather's change in demeanor.

"But you always cry."

"I cry because I am sick I tell you," he spat again and cursed bitterly in Italian.

Nigel watched his mother move about the kitchen as she prepared another large meal for the three of them. He was making her nervous he could tell. She looked at him occasionally from the corner of her eye.

"So you were what…seventeen?" he asked finally. She looked at him with confusion heavily showing on her face.

"Seventeen? Yeah I've been seventeen once…maybe twice," she chuckled.

"I mean when I was born," he said.

As she continued to knead the bread dough, Nigel could almost see the cogs of her mind turning.

"Yeah, seventeen. What is up with this conversation Nigel?"

"And that name Nigel, what kind of Italian is named Nigel Godwins. Everybody thinks I'm Jewish or something," he continued to badger her.

"Well you're not a Jew you are an Italian just like your mother…"

"…and like my father?" he interjected. She glared at him and then looked around him for her father, who had disappeared into his room.

"Honey what is going on?" she asked, as she washed her hands and dried them on the apron she wore. "Why do you talk to me like this?"

"Because I'm thirty-six years old and I'm about to be a father and I've been lied to my whole life about my father."

"Who told you this? Oh, my god; your grandfather told you. I can't believe he betrayed me this way." Her eyes filled with tears.

"Ma, cut the drama, please." Nigel's voice rose just a little. She stood quiet.

"So this other Nigel Godwins person who is supposed to be my father, who is he?" he asked her.

She looked out the window and then back at him. His hazel eyes bore a hold in her heart. She felt tired now, beaten a little. Suddenly, she saw the face of the man; she so often wanted to forget, on her son. She often forced herself to deny any resemblance between Nigel and his father.

"He was a married man…and he didn't die on the way to the hospital," she said sounding defeated. Nigel swallowed hard. "What did your papa tell you?" she asked.

"Not much. He started crying, but he told me my father isn't dead. So who is he?"

"Well, he isn't dead," she said and then led him into the dining room. She cleared the table of the floral centerpiece and motioned for him to sit, which he did without taking his eyes off her.

"At seventeen you think you know everything," she began. "But I didn't know nothing," she continued. "I remember my mother telling me the day you came, 'Marcela, this war you are having with this man you will never win, only God will win.'" she said.

As she told Nigel her story, for the first time Nigel cried. He didn't know why the story had driven him to tears but for the first time he thought perhaps he could understand now why his grandfather always cried. On the surface it didn't seem like such a horrible story…what his father had done, considering who he was. But in the big picture it made Nigel feel so empty inside. It made him feel bought and paid for, like an umbrella you would buy in a store and only need when it rained. Any other time, you would simply put it away and not give it a second thought.

She had made a wager with all that she had to offer and lost. Nigel's grandmother had called it a wager against God and in those types of bets only God can win…therefore he was named…Godwins.

Not only wasn't his father named Nigel Godwins, he wasn't Italian. He was a white man that while his mother trusted him with her love, her body, and her life he deceived her led her on. Knowing he was committed to a life that included money and success, he conceived a child with Marcela, Nigel's mother. He made promises to be there for her. He had told her he loved her. He had even given her the name Nigel, after his own father, to give the child if it was a son. But then suddenly he changed, like a change in weather he blew her off when the time came for her to give birth. He just suddenly planned on forgetting about her, as if she and the baby would just go away and there was no explanation.

Marcela figured it had to have been some type of pressure from his wife's family and the thought of losing all he had accumulated by marrying into her money. Finally it was only through threats from Nigel's grandfather that this man did the right thing…

"If that's what you want to call it. He knew we couldn't afford to get any better lawyer than he already was, so…I guess he felt sorry for me. Sure he paid for things as time went on…your education and with his influence and history with old man Madison he had even gotten you the job with Madison and Associates," Marcela explained.

"But it wasn't the money that made it bad. It was how I felt taking it. I felt like a whore. He made me feel like one the way he only came around when he was down or he wanted to sneak a peek at you. He made me feel like I was a business. Like I was where he stored his child until he needed one. You can't make a child a convenient business."

His mother cried now as she spoke of the feelings she had. "I didn't even feel like I could marry. I loved him so much and I had to just 'get over it'. I'm a Catholic! My father and mother were so ashamed of me. They told me to tell everyone your father had died. So I did. I even told you that. Finally I had to accept what was not going to change and make a life for you, a new life. For a while, as the years went by and he got more successful on his own he started coming around more and it got actually better for a short time. I think he felt ashamed of how he had abandoned me. But he wouldn't divorce his wife, and I hate him for that. They even had a family; you have a brother and a sister. I finally made him stop coming around because he had started coming to your little games at the school and I didn't want you to know him…and sneaking around your concerts, when you played that horn…remember that horn you played?" she smiled touching his face; he nodded.

"Nigel if you don't have nothing else to do with this woman, now that you know who she is, be a father to your child. Be more than a check. Don't make this baby a business deal. Don't be like your father. See if you can dig deep inside and find some real feelings. He's dead to you now. You are a better man than he is, I know it," his mother said, as he stood on the step readying to leave.

She spoke so simplistically.

Perhaps she really had no idea how she had changed his life this day. He knew he would have to confront his father now, he would have to see why, even now, he continued to sneak in and out of his life, touching it the way one brushes up against a stranger in a crowd. But first he would have to change some things with Qiana. He realized now, he too had made a wager against God the day he entered that clinic and the odds of winning this bet weren't looking too good for him.

He could hear the Marconi's baby crying again tonight.

Qiana peeked out the window and saw the BMW parked out front. It was nearly ten p.m. She debated whether or not to open the door but with his constant banging she knew she would have to as he had no intention of ending it anytime soon.

"What do you want?" she said sharply. Nigel looked around uncomfortably.

"Can I come in?"

"Hell no," she said flatly.

"Ok, fine. I'm sorry about this afternoon. And I want to try something else, ok?"

"Something else like what?" she asked cautiously.

"Ok, since you are insisting on going through with this and I will never understand why. I mean especially now that you know it's me..." he chuckled nervously, in that way that Qiana found so cute. "Anyway, let me help you."

"I don't need your help."

"Yes, you do; look at this place. It's not a place to raise a baby. It's small and this neighborhood is bad," he said, having noticed the derelicts hanging out on the corner. "Let me help you get moved and situated," he offered. Slowly the door opened and he stepped inside.

She had furnished the small apartment the best she could. It showed care and time but he knew she was struggling.

"Was that your mom that uh...I sorta met today?" he said looking around.

"Yes," she said clicking on a small lamp and tightening her robe belt around her waist.

"I thought pregnant women were like...pregnant," he said, noticing her thin waist and holding his hands several inches away from his midriff.

"Oh, I'm not showing much yet, well I think I am but..." She stopped speaking abruptly. What was she doing letting him in her world this way? "What do you want Nigel?" she asked curtly.

"Tomorrow I wanna pick you up and we can go look for a nicer place…" he began.

He knew it was coming out wrong. Even before her face showed the irritation, he could hear his own words. He raised his hands in surrender. "Anyway, a bigger place, a safer place, a house with a yard. Like where I grew up and…"

"Like where I grew up," she said softly as she began to look around her apartment. She had never liked it but it was near her job and it was within her price range.

Her sister Chalice had a good job and lived in a house, but she lived with two other girls and they split everything. And soon she and Marvin would be getting married and he had a good job too.

Russell had never been much help and it had been hard supporting the both of them.

Her decision to have this baby was not thought out past the initial payment of the procedure. She really didn't know how she was going to afford everything her child would need. Reality had been biting her hard lately. She hadn't told anyone…not even Rashawn.

"Ok," she said. "But what will I have to do?"

"Nothing. And I want *it* to have my name…I don't mean *it*, I mean, him or her," he corrected himself.

"Godwins?" Qiana stammered. Nigel nodded without making eye contact with her and continued to speak quickly without giving her many chances to say anything. He began to explain how it should all go…this partnership of theirs.

This was happening too fast.

"The money is not an issue, so you call me when you need anything…better yet." He pulled out his wallet. Qiana held up her hand to stop him.

"No, listen…I want to do this. You're not a whore," he said without looking at her. He didn't notice her face or the expression of total amazement at his candor, which bordered just a little bit on the side audacity.

She was taken aback by this strange man...so rude and yet underneath, he really did seem to care. "I just want to make it easy." He handed her his credit card. "Now tomorrow I will call and get you on as an authorized user."

"Why are you trusting me? You are a lawyer and this is so dumb for you to do."

"You'll never understand. I don't understand, really. It was something my grandmother said. Let's just say, this ain't the Superbowl," he chuckled at what seemed to be a profound yet, very private revelation. "But hey, you abuse it and I'll just close the account and chalk it up to bad judgment," he smiled at her. "What is your last name?"

"Patterson. Qiana A. Patterson."

"What's the A for?"

"Alisani," she answered.

"Alisani. That's pretty."

"My grandmother's name," she said.

"My grandmother's name was Ana," Nigel said.

"That's a pretty name too," Qiana said.

And so the small talk went until four or five a.m.

Accepting all that was yet to come was going to be little bit tougher though...he could tell. But Qiana had made it easy, in just those few hours of talking; she had put him at ease about so many things, actually that was almost the most un-nerving part of this whole thing...She had made it almost too easy to accept all that was happening.

Nigel woke up covered by a Kente printed quilt. He realized then, he was still in Qiana's apartment. He noticed the time. It was at about eight a.m. The phone rang and on the third ring he heard Qiana's voice as the answering machine picked up.

"Qiana girl, its Rashawn. What is going on? Nigel said he was going to talk to you about things. Well did he? Did he? Girlfriend...where are you at?" The casual and playful, one-sided phone conversation ended and knowing Rashawn, as he felt he had grown to, she was no doubt on her way over.

Nigel folded the quilt and laid it neatly over the back of the sofa. He noticed the credit card still on the coffee table where he had put it last night. He knew then, that he had made the right decision; she was in no hurry to rip him off. He locked her door before closing it behind him.

He felt good inside that at least one of the disruptions to his life had been nipped in the bud. Today he felt in total control. He hated feeling out of control.

Tomorrow was another story...

Court adjourned promptly and Winston Montgomery disappeared quickly into his chambers. Nigel wondered if perhaps he had forgotten the appointment that the two of them had for this afternoon.

He had made the appointment stating it was a private matter...It bordered more on an emergency, but Nigel had kept his cool with the Judge's secretary, when he called to make the appointment earlier that morning.

Getting to see a judge was hard enough without sounding mysterious. It was bad enough he was with the firm representing his wife, in what was turning into a very nasty divorce, now he had a private matter to discuss.

Nigel had been hearing rumors that the Judge was behind the efforts to have him represented out of the divorce case...removed entirely from the proceedings...so he knew Judge Montgomery would surely think he knew what this visit was concerning. What else could it possibly be about? Nigel nervously began to reason that perhaps Judge Montgomery would pretend he didn't know...making it seem as though he wanted to argue with him about being removed from the divorce proceedings...perhaps he would simply dismiss him without thinking twice. Nigel had to see him. He couldn't let it go...it would have to be resolved now! He was panicking now...he thoughts were all over the place.

He took a deep breath as he knocked on the chamber door.

He heard the invite to 'come on in' and Judge Montgomery had even called him by his first name...he began to think that perhaps he had been wrong about the ol Albino.

"Have a seat, Nigel," the Judge said and a smile actually crossed his face. Nigel had never been this close to him before and it made him uncomfortable, the way his almost white eyes, locked on him.

Now, in the presence of his father, after dreaming of this moment his whole life, Nigel didn't know to say.

"I'm sure you must have some questions," Winston Montgomery asked. Nigel could think of only one...

What had his mother seen in him?

CHAPTER 12

Terrell noticed a lighter mood in Nigel over the next few weeks and it may him curious. He seemed more confident and almost happy. Terrell couldn't figure it out. He had been represented out…removed entirely from the Montgomery divorce case and it didn't even bother him. This wasn't like Nigel to take something like that lying down.

Terrell knew he would have to get to the bottom of his friend's strange new behavior. He could have sworn he had even seen Nigel look slightly irritated with him when he referred to the Judge as 'that ol Albino'. Since when did Nigel get defensive over any snide remark about one of the judges?

"So what choo doing tonight?" He called out over the parking lot. Nigel looked around trying to find the direction of Terrell's voice. He noticed him and smiled.

"Gotta go shopping," he called back.

He knew the vagueness of his reply would puzzle Terrell.

"Shopping…like groceries?"

"No, more like a shopping date," Nigel answered sounding almost mysterious. He noticed Terrell re-lock his car and start towards him.

"Did I hear date? Thought I would never hear that word outta you, again" he sounded intrigued.

"I knew you'd want to get all nosy with that one. I'm surprised that Rita didn't tell you all about it," Nigel said in a tone, mocking children spilling a secret.

"I've been busy."

"Well then I guess you haven't noticed the house down the street from Rita's, with that, 'In Escrow' sign on it."

"Haven't paid attention, why?"

"I bought it," Nigel grinned.

"You're moving to *The Palemos*?" Terrell's eyes widened.

"Naw, I got it for Qiana and the baby," he said sounding causal, like it was an everyday thing—buying a house for a pregnant girl that he hardly knew.

"You bought Qiana a house?"

"Well she's gonna pay rent; I'm the landlord." He pretended to pull on invisible suspenders.

What was happening to his once tight-pocketed sensible friend? Terrell couldn't believe Nigel had already given Qiana free reign with his credit card—What was next?

"You sleeping with her?" Terrell asked. Nigel frowned.

"No, I'm not sleeping with her; she's pregnant," Nigel said, as if sex with a pregnant woman was the wildest concept for anyone to have thought up.

"But if she wasn't pregnant you'd be sleeping with her?"

"If she wasn't pregnant I wouldn't be buying the house."

"Oh, so it's only because of the baby you're doing all this?"

"Well, I guess, yes," Nigel finally admitted.

"And that's what I told Rita," Terrell said with self-confirmation in his tone.

Nigel suddenly realized he didn't like how that sounded but it was the truth. All of this was for the baby's sake and Qiana knew it too. They had talked about it. There were no secrets; but still, it sounded awful.

"The house went into escrow today," Nigel said to Qiana just the day before, during dinner. He had gotten the green light from the Realtor that morning and couldn't wait to tell her.

"That was fast," she said.

She felt uncomfortable about this whole thing but didn't quite know how to bring up the issue of the house and ownership and the strings that were ever so tightly becoming attached. She had talked it over with her parents, who were both so excited they failed to be very objective.

"So, when do I move in?" she said.

"It won't be long now but I'll let you know. I mean, I will have to get the keys and the contracts and stuff," he smiled.

"Contracts?"

"Yeah, so we don't have any confusion over anything. I mean, I don't want any confusion."

"Confusion?"

"Yeah, like landlord tenant stuff. It's not the most pleasant part of this whole thing, but it has to happen. I mean, this is for the baby and everything but we can't get lost in that kind of emotion," he added. "I mean, when I have a key I wouldn't want you to get all weird."

"I wouldn't, but I'm glad you are thinking about stuff like that. I mean, you are just the landlord and I'm just the tenant," she said in a determined tone.

"Yep and we just happen to have a baby," Nigel smiled.

Qiana thought about what he had just said…*we.*

She hadn't thought about it ever being a *'we' when she had made up her mind to get a baby this way.*

Later at the mall Nigel and Qiana enjoyed their 'mall date', as Terrell called it.

"I hate that some people act like people can't just do stuff for each other without sleeping together. Like, people can't have a business arrangement like ours…that bugs me," Qiana commented, once again reminding herself where there they stood in regards to each other.

It was true that Nigel had called nearly every night to, supposedly, talk about the house and that usually they just ended up talking for hours about everything from general things to deeper issues and current events. He wanted to know how she was feeling, what the doctor was saying…Despite her constant confirmations to herself of being simply a platonic relationship between them, the line was growing blurrier everyday.

"I'll get that," he said as he handed the counter girl the dollar for the ice cream cone. Qiana smiled; just a little embarrassed that she had ordered such a large one; if she had known he was going to pay she would have ordered the smaller cone.

"Thanks," she said.

They strolled on into the mall until they came to *Baby World*. Nigel looked in the display window, all the pink and blues of this and that. He had no way of knowing that such a little person would require so many things.

He followed Qiana into the store. He watched her expression, as she too looked at all the things hanging and displayed. She seemed overwhelmed as well.

The clerk approached them, smiling brightly.

"Hello there, may I help you find something you need?" She sounded perky and ready to assist. "Is this your first baby?" she said addressing them both. They stood in awkward silence for a moment.

"Yes," Qiana finally said. "It's my first. I wanted to look at some baby cribs and things."

"Well you two come this way." She smiled again.

After looking over the cribs and bassinets, Nigel had to admit he hadn't seen anything that caught his eye.

Though his mother hadn't spoken him directly since the day he had found out about his father, his grandfather had told him that she had spent days locked in the attic 'digging around' as he called it.

"I think she's doing something with the family cradle," he said.

Nigel knew immediately this was to be a grand gift as that cradle had been in his family for four generations. The bed had been made by hand, carved out of cherry wood and unblemished by time and wear. Nigel had even slept in it. He couldn't believe it was actually coming to him as an inheritance.

His mother had over reacted with tears and emotion, when he told had her he had actually gone and met his father. It was the same day he informed her that Qiana was indeed going to go through with the pregnancy and that it was indeed, going to a business arrangement…no bones about it.

She had not spoken to him directly since, so he had no way of knowing which issue she was still reacting to…*the meeting his father…or turning into his father*, part. He knew he had overwhelmed her and she just needed time. So when his grandfather called and confirmed to him that she was indeed working on the cradle for the baby he knew she would get over it soon.

"Why were you being so difficult in there? There had to be at least eighty bassinets to choose from. It was *Baby World* for crying out loud," Qiana said with mild irritation showing in her tone as they left the store. Nigel took the small bag from her, smiling that…'*I could care less that you are irritated with me*,' smile of his. They had managed to find a few things, but not much.

"That store stunk. It didn't have anything good. Plus everything was green or yellow. When do you know what color to buy? Isn't it suppose to be like blue or pink?" he asked, as she rolled her eyes. She could see he was in a playful mood.

"That store is one of the best baby stores in the city," she said trying to keep him focused and serious.

"Depending on your taste," he remarked sarcastically and started to walk on.

"And what does that mean?" She stood her ground.

Nigel wasn't going to give in to this one. They had been bickering over silly things for about a week. They were beginning to remind him of Terrell and Rita, the way they would get in such heated debates over nothing, only to end up with Qiana saying she had won...no matter what.

He found himself calling her every night to resolve something they had bickered over the day before. It was addicting; he sort of liked it.

Qiana didn't whine like Sherry did. She didn't slam doors or get hateful in her tone. With Qiana, Nigel could always tell it wasn't really an 'argument' as her defense was always so weak and illogical.

He had never been in a male-female relationship where he felt so free to agree to disagree. He had never felt free to make his point to the bitter end with anyone and still remain good friends, other than Terrell. He now found that he enjoyed going the rounds with Qiana.

"Ok, I'm gonna bet you that I can find a something of better quality than any bed in there," he said haughtily and with confidence, taunting her.

"Oh and if I win?" She put her hand on what was left of her waistline.

"To show you how confident I am, if I lose, I will kiss your ass." He leaned close to her face. Her eyes widened at his boorish remark.

"And if I lose, oh, I'm suppose to kiss yours?" she said biting the inside of her cheek to hold back from grinning. "Oh, that's too easy." Her face was on fire now, and it had to have shown.

This wasn't as easy as when they were on the phone. She could say just about anything to him and he never had to see her blush.

They had given in to light flirtation, but only over the phone. Qiana knew her hormones were raging now, as she felt sexually driven constantly. It was hard to fight her urgings when Nigel would say certain things or look at her certain ways. Sometimes she could swear he could sense the lust she was feeling for him.

Just then, Nigel heard his name called by a familiar voice. He turned from Qiana's face, only to come face to face with Sherry and she was with James.

Sherry's eyes widened, as she looked Qiana over.

Qiana's hair was pulled tight on her head in a bun. And she wore no makeup. She was glowing and beautiful, as that bulge under that big shirt could not be hidden. Sherry's heart sank; although, she hid it well behind her tight smile.

"Qiana, I'm surprised to see you're still…well, pregnant," Sherry began. Her words came out worse sounding than she had planed but she couldn't take them back now. She was hurt and all was up for grabs. She was a dirty fighter and worse so when her feelings were at stake. "Honey, this is the girl that Nigel artificially inseminated. I told you about her."

Qiana grew more and more uncomfortable with every second. Nigel noticed immediately and became instantly determined to end this showdown before it went any further…Qiana didn't deserve this.

"Sherry, stop," Nigel said in a cool even tone; one that used to signal the end of a discussion, but Sherry looked over it tonight.

"Wow, seeing you two together, what a shock," Sherry continued in her jealous vent. Nigel had never seen her attack so quickly before. "You make a cute couple Nigel. Are you two together now?" she finally added.

"Stop," Nigel said again holding up his hand to her face. He looked at James, who appeared quite helpless. "I really don't have to explain myself to you?" Nigel added.

Not wanting to say anything to hurt or embarrass Qiana, he knew he should just walk away but he couldn't resist one more dig at her.

"I have to say you really don't wear 'Jealous Bitch' well, Sherry," he said in a cool low tone, speaking directly to her. He could have sworn he saw her eyes tighten as if now fighting back emotion.

"Sherry sweetie, maybe Nigel and his friend would like to continue in their little shopping spree. I mean they do…"

"*Baby World*? Oh Nigel there is a much better baby store, downtown. Matter a fact it's near *Family Makers*," Sherry interrupted again; in her last ditch effort to come out of the confrontation with some pride left.

Qiana had had enough; she slid her arm around Nigel's waist.

"Well baby, I guess I lost the bet then and tonight I'll be kissing *your* ass for a change," Qiana said, her comment dripping with sarcasm. Nigel looked at her, shocked at her retort. It made him smile.

"Yeah, I guess so," he said winking at her and flashing a devilish smile.

Qiana attempted the best she could to saunter away from the small group and disappeared into *Beatrice's Drawers*, the lingerie store.

"None of that was necessary, Sherry," Nigel said looking back towards the store that Qiana had gone into. "Better watch her James, she can be a real witch sometimes," Nigel added mocking true concern for his feelings.

Sherry eyes once again were sharp and darting. "Now if you will excuse me I have to go help her pick out some panties." Nigel added, grinning slyly as he walked away.

Later, at the restaurant near the mall, Qiana thought about the confrontation at the mall.

"I am so sorry I said that. I don't know what got into me," she said as she looked over the menu.

"No, I'm sorry. I don't know why all that happened. I have never seen Sherry like that. That's a lie; I've seen her like that a lot; just never directed at me. But it's ok," he said.

"It would have been worse if it had been my ex though. If I had pretended we were together, there would have been some drama."

"You didn't tell me you had an ex," Nigel said sounding truly interested. Qiana looked up from her menu. She hadn't planed on discussing Russell with him. She had tried not to think about him much.

"Oh, we were together for like three or four years; until the baby."

"Was it a good relationship? I guess that's dumb to ask." Nigel thought about her decision to have a baby the way she had.

"He had changed. I sometimes was even a little afraid of him," she chuckled nervously.

"Afraid?" Nigel asked as the waitress brought water and they ordered dinner.

"He hit me once or twice," she said not looking at him.

"Not once...but twice?" Nigel's tone was that of an attorney now.

"Well, it wasn't anything really. It's over now." Qiana smiled and took a cleansing breath.

She had a very warm smile and Nigel enjoyed looking at it. It made him feel good somewhere deep inside. He could tell she didn't want to talk about this ex anymore and he wouldn't push it.

"Now about this ass kissing," he said in a half effort to flirt. Qiana frowned and looked at him.

"I said I was sorry." She was serious now.

"I was kidding Qiana, lighten up," he said filling his mouth with pasta. "This is nothing like my ma's cooking. Man, that woman can cook some pasta."

"Nigel, I need to say something ok?" Qiana began slowly.

"Yeah."

"Now don't get all mad or weird."

"Yeah."

"I don't want a relationship with you. I mean, I just want to be friends," Qiana began. "You have to understand. I had planned on having this baby myself. I hadn't planned on sharing. And now you have just come into my life and I don't know, I seem to losing my..."

"Control," he said finishing her sentence. She nodded.

"Don't get me wrong I think you are a nice guy but I just don't want to be with you in that way," she added.

Nigel didn't know if he felt hurt or relieved. He just looked at her for moment and then continued eating.

"Ok?" she asked, trying to make eye contact with him.

"Then we need some rules," he finally said after a couple of minutes of silence. "Like a contract," he added.

"Well, I didn't mean to…"

"No, we need a contract," he said, taking a napkin from the holder. He held his hand out for a pen. She dug in her purse to find one and then handed it to him.

"Number one: No google eye making," he said. She began to giggle.

"Number two," he began with a straight face. "None of that cute giggling and stuff," he said, holding back a smile.

"Number three," she blurted. "No green shirt wearing."

She was referring to the hunter green shirt he now wore that made his eyes so wonderfully colored that she could barely keep herself from staring. He looked puzzled for a moment and then wrote it down.

"No green shirt wearing," he smiled.

"Number fifty, no kissing," she said as they walked together up to her door.

"I'm running out of napkin," Nigel joked as he attempted to scribble yet another 'rule' onto the napkin from the restaurant.

They had laughed and made rules guarding them from their growing feelings all evening. Qiana opened the door.

"Wanna come inside?" she offered, sounding out of breath from laughter. Nigel looked over the napkin on both sides.

"It's not on here so I guess so," he smiled. Just then her face lit up. She took his hand and laid it on her stomach.

"I don't know if you can feel it. I have been feeling the baby kick for a couple weeks now," she smiled.

She and Nigel now stood perfectly still to wait for the next movement or sign of life. But the baby was still now.

"Missed it," Nigel finally sighed.

"Next time," she said still holding his hand on her stomach.

Their eyes were fixed on each other's and as their lips grew closer Qiana closed her eyes. Suddenly Nigel pulled back.

"Qiana! No kissing," he said, totally tongue in cheek.

"I'm sorry," she said sounding very embarrassed. He kissed her anyway.

"I'm sorry," he smiled.

Just then he felt the movement…ever so fleeting, his baby moved inside her.

"Oh man, I felt it!" he exploded in excitement. His giddiness made her giggle.

"Can I stay for a while at least until it happens again. I'll leave after, I promise," he requested.

"Boy for someone who didn't want any part of this you are really getting into it."

"I know, I don't get it," Nigel said exposing his feelings to her a little more than he had planned.

They lay together in Qiana's bed fully dressed in the darkened bedroom. Nigel, with his hand on her stomach, eagerly anticipated the baby's movement. He was not disappointed.

The next morning Qiana awoke and found herself wrapped tightly in Nigel's arms. Still fully dressed, but feeling awkward and embarrassed, she attempted to slide out from under his arm without waking him, but failed. He sat up and quickly climbed off the bed, rumpled and half-awake. She could tell he wasn't a morning person.

Without saying anything he sat on the edge of the bed smoothing back his hair and putting on his shoes.

"I'll call you later," he said, yawing and stretching as he started out of the bedroom

As she watched him, all her embarrassment passed; he was just Nigel, the man who once thought he didn't want anything or anyone in his world except his job.

He had somehow crowded himself into her life and she couldn't get him out…not even if she wanted to.

When she heard her front door close behind him, she pulled down her blanket and climbed under the covers and slept until noon.

Later Nigel called.

"So what's your week looking like?"

"Oh, I have an appointment Monday morning; it's an ultrasound. I'm going before work."

"What's that gonna do?" he asked.

"You're not reading that book are you?" she reprimanded. He sat quiet on his end.

"I uh…no. So just answer me."

"Well, I'm hoping tomorrow I find out the baby's sex. I got one before but we were sort of still guessing. We are hoping that the baby is flash dancing tomorrow and exposing his little stuff so we can tell," she giggled.

"His little *stuff*? How embarrassing, poor guy; everybody standing around looking for his *stuff*."

"Well there might not be any…*stuff*."

"And then what will that mean?" Nigel sounded sincere.

"It will mean *he's* a she," Qiana laughed. Nigel chuckled at his ignorance.

"Now this is a thing I can relate to; getting to some real answers."

"Well…"

"Well what? You mean I can go?" he asked.

"Oh of course, you are the father," her voice softened.

Nigel sat quiet for a moment. Qiana began to think that maybe she had intimidated him with that comment.

"I would like to come with you Monday," he finally said.

"Meet me at the hospital," she said.

Qiana's bladder was full for the ultra sound, uncomfortably so.

"I hope this isn't going too take long," she said, trying not to giggle. Doctor Young smiled at Nigel, shaking his hand cordially and then turned his attention back to her.

"So, Qiana tells me you sort of accidentally ended up being a part of this experience?" he asked not looking at Nigel directly.

"Yeah, you could say that," Nigel answered.

"Well, trust me its going to be an experience of a lifetime." Doctor Young smiled and handed him a stethoscope.

Nigel couldn't believe what he was hearing. The tiny heartbeat could be heard going, what seemed to be a hundred miles an hour.

"Wow, this is fantastic." He grinned broadly at Qiana who was touched by his excitement.

"But that's nothing," the Doctor added.

The monitor was ready now and together they looked at the picture that was easily seen.

Nigel, without realizing what he was doing, held on tight to Qiana's hand as the doctor scanned the fetus, finding head, arms, legs, and the absence of a penis. It was the picture of their little girl.

"Now Qiana, here is the video to blackmail your teenage daughter with on her first date," Doctor Young chuckled as he handed her the tape of what had been seen on the monitor. Nigel intercepted her receiving it.

"Uh, I would like to make a copy of this and I will give one to you tonight," he said to her.

The doctor was a little embarrassed now, at how he had so easily counted Nigel out of the experience of the morning, after telling him what a wonderful one it would be. He chuckled nervously.

"Oh my, I'm sorry Mr. Godwins, I didn't think…" Doctor Young stumbled.

"No, no problem. And you can call me Nigel." He smoothed back his hair before looking at Qiana who hadn't said anything, as her heart was so full of tender affection for him at this moment.

"This was the coolest morning," Nigel said to Terrell that afternoon over lunch. He was bubbly and in a good mood.

"What was so cool about it? It's Monday for goodness sake," Terrell growled. Nigel laughed out loud…louder than he intended too. Terrell looked at him with a flat expression. "What's got you all goofy today?"

"It's a girl," Nigel said in a half whisper.

Terrell turned around thinking he was about to see some new female interest of Nigel's. There was no one but Hairy Larry cleaning off the tables.

"What girl?"

"The baby, it's a girl," Nigel said. Terrell put his hand to his mouth in mock surprise.

"Oh the *bay bee*," he squealed, his voice once again imitating falsetto, mocking and sarcastic.

"Oh stop, you just wait until you hear an, 'unborn's' heartbeat man; you wait. You won't feel so tough. It's a humbling thing," Nigel said sounding quite proud.

"But what about you and Qiana? Rita won't tell me anything."

"That is because there is nothing to tell," Nigel frowned.

"Ok great. Let's get together this evening and…"

"Oh, I uh was gonna be cooking tonight for Qiana. She's coming over for the first time," Nigel admitted sheepishly. Terrell rolled his eyes.

"Come on in." Nigel swung open the door wide. Qiana stepped onto the hardwood threshold. Though she could see the attempts at warmth, the place appeared fresh out of a magazine for home beautiful…complete with the attached price tags.

"Smells great," she said inhaling the aroma drifting from the kitchen. She could tell already he was a good cook and the meal would be perfect. On the stove, every large pot was filled with something bubbling and rich looking.

With one click of his remote control, the air filled with smooth jazz.

"I'd dim the lights with this button here, but then we wouldn't be able to see," he chuckled, as he continued to set the small bistro table in the kitchen with a place setting for two. Qiana had hoped they weren't going to be eating at that large dining room monstrosity that she passed on her way into the kitchen.

He poured milk into a crystal goblet and sat it in front of her and then, throwing a white cup towel over his arm he took her order.

She clapped as he juggled the garlic press and pepper mill...it was turning into quite a delightful evening.

After eating they went back into the living room.

"This is a very nice place," Qiana said, as she looked around at his nick-knacks on the shelves.

"Oh you haven't seen the half of it." He reached out for her hand. "The tour begins," he invited.

Qiana took his hand as he led her down the hall, showing her the spare rooms, closets and office.

Soon they approached his bedroom. He went in, but she stood in the doorway peeking in.

The room was surprisingly simple.

"It used to be fancier in here but...you know, it was a girly room. So I got a new bed and dresser and stuff," he said, pointing out the replaced items. Qiana noticed the framed pictures on his dresser, and they drew her inside. She was curious to see pictures of any relatives of his.

One picture, taken New Year's Eve, was of Rita and Terrell and Nigel. She picked it up to get a closer look. There was the cut off portion of an arm around Nigel's shoulder. Qiana assumed it to be Sherry's. Suddenly Nigel grabbed the picture from her.

"Creative scanning," he chuckled and replaced that picture in her hand with an older looking one. "Now this is Ana," he said referring to the old photo of his grandmother. "I revamped it on my computer. It's really old," he said proudly. She was impressed.

There was a quiet moment between them. Their eyes locked. Nigel noticed now she had worn no make-up, but was incredibly beautiful.

"Qiana," he began, but then kissed her instead of speaking.

"The rules Nigel," Qiana said returning the kiss.

"I'm sorry," he lied, kissing her again. The deep kiss filled him with passion and he became aroused.

"I don't think we covered this one on that napkin," she said softly.

"Good thing," he said, smiling broadly.

They wasted no time making it into Nigel's bed. Qiana's natural shyness was instantly gone as she, without inhibition, gave into all she was feeling during his slow and deliberate foreplay. Nigel grew completely familiar with her body as he explored, causing sensations all too new for the both of them.

After the passion they lay quiet, soaking up the moment. It was as if both knew tomorrow they would return to being 'just friends' and they wanted this moment, spent as lovers, to last a little longer.

"The baby is kicking," Qiana said, taking Nigel's hand and lying it on her bare stomach. He felt the movement and then kissed her stomach.

"Sorry about the headache," he said, directing the comment towards her belly. Qiana burst into laughter and playfully pushed his head away.

Moving day had come. Nigel and Terrell had been sent down to Los Angeles for a commencement ceremony at one of the law schools there. Luis had asked them to speak at his alumni and it made it seem like an honor and the two of them were glad to do it for him. Qiana assured him that it would be fine as Charles and her father had the moving thing under control.

It indeed had turned into an exciting and busy day, but also, the day that Qiana was hit with her first bout of morning sickness.

"You know, I was the same way. I never got sick until the middle of my pregnancy. It was the strangest thing," Daphne said calmly, as all waited for Qiana to finish up in the bathroom before they could continue working. She was insisting that she wanted to be helpful, but instead of helping, her trips to the bathroom had only slowed them. They had gotten at least an hour behind schedule. Qiana's father had already left to coach a soccer game.

"Qiana, do you think we could pick this up at the new house," Charles said through the door to the bathroom. He was losing patience with her; Selena glared at him.

"Charles leave her alone. She didn't plan this."

"Where are Nigel and Terrell?" He showed his irritation.

"They are out of town on business," Qiana answered, as she swaggered from the bathroom. She looked exhausted already and they had yet to make one trip to the new house.

"How convenient," Charles barked. Qiana started to cry and Charles was immediately sorry.

"I didn't mean it Qi, it's just I'm not quite ready for this invisible man thing. I mean, he gives you a baby, he gives you a house, and he gives you...I don't know. What happened to love and..." Charles shook his head and grabbed up a heavy box. "I just can't get into this anymore. We haven't even met him," he said. Qiana cried even more.

"I met him briefly once," Daphne remarked as she carried the lamp out to the truck.

When they reached the house in *The Palemos*, Rashawn and some of her cousins were waiting outside.

Selena squealed when she noticed the white picket fence. "This is the cutest house I have ever seen." The snapdragons grew wild and nearly covered the walkway up to the front door. There was a large front window.

Qiana remembered when she and Nigel first saw the house together with the Realtor this window was what she had loved most about it.

She opened the front door with the key and they all walked in. In the middle of the empty living room, there it sat the most perfect gift.

Nigel's mother had finished restoring the cradle. She had dolled it up with pink bows and fluffy comforters, stuffed animals and such.

She hadn't been speaking to Nigel since the day he had gone to meet his father and told her about it. She had been overwhelmed with too much at one time. The news of the baby and Qiana's decision to keep it and Winston Montgomery's name coming up after so long a time…it had been too much for her.

Over the last few weeks, Nigel had called his grandfather a few times to ask what he should do about his mother's attitude towards him. He seemed to have a normal enough solution…for grandpa.

"Just let her stew in it," was all he said.

But after Nigel called and told his grandfather that the baby was to be a girl, apparently he had passed that information over to his mother. She worked through her issues and soon had made the perfect offering.

He hugged her and she responded to his affections with tears; all was forgiven.

He had used his key to go into the house that morning; he and Terrell set up the cradle before leaving to Los Angeles.

Walking over to the cradle now, with all its balloons and pink bows, her heart filled, nearly to capacity. But it wasn't until she saw the card and read it, that she no longer could contain her emotions…

"For Ana," was all it said…but that was enough, Qiana cried the rest of the afternoon.

CHAPTER 13

Time was flying by but so many things stayed the same.

"So tell me again, you're on a boat with some party animals," Smithy repeated, as he bounced the tennis balls looking for the most buoyant one.

"No, now you don't listen," Terrell snapped. "He hears the boat and then he sees the people on the lookout."

"And then the black chick. Is she still a black chick?"

"Yes! Now you have never heard him say anything except that she's a black chick. He has had this dream a hunnered times." Terrell served the ball and Nigel returned it. "So is she all moved in?" Terrell asked Nigel.

"Yeah. I think that is going to be real nice her living there near Rashawn and stuff," Nigel said, as the play continued.

"Yeah, that's gonna be real nice. Especially since Rita and me are getting married and she won't be living there with Rashawn anymore," Terrell said, catching Nigel by surprise. The tennis ball whizzed by his head.

"Set and match," Smithy called out, as he and Nigel switched places on the court.

"You and Rita are getting married? When?" Nigel asked. Terrell grinned and looked almost boyish, in his innocence.

"I figured it was time. I mean, it's not like there's been anybody else for me...ever," Terrell reasoned out loud.

Nigel gave the words a moment of deep thought.

"Back to that dream Nigel…have you ever thought that perhaps it's the song that is in question? That perhaps in that song there is hidden meaning there, in the words?" Smithy pondered, as he bounced the ball again, readying to challenge Terrell who was still hyper from beating Nigel without much effort.

"The song has no words," Nigel added. "Twenty-Love," he called out as Terrell torn into Smithy.

He was an aggressive player and always won.

Meanwhile the girls spent the morning together back at Qiana's house.

"Girl, your belly is really getting out there." Rita patted Qiana's stomach. "I want a baby," she sighed and then rubbed her own belly. "For good luck," she grinned.

Rashawn brought in another box from the car.

"Please, you have Terrell," Rashawn laughed. "And Qiana has Nigel…and all this stuff," she sighed heavily, as they looked around at the things bought on the last shopping spree. The girls then giggled under their breath.

"I cannot believe he helped you pick out all this stuff," Rita asked. Qiana nodded, looking sheepish.

"Yeah and what's this about dinner tonight at your folks?" Rashawn asked. Qiana now felt on the spot.

"My parents want to meet him. There are no strings attached. He said he would do this for me, no big deal." Qiana shrugged her shoulders in a seemingly nonchalant manner.

"Girlfriend, don't you see what's happening; all this baby stuff and this house; he is falling for you."

"No, he isn't. We have become friends. We actually like each other a lot; as friends," she added.

The sisters winked at one another, as they both were certain they had caught Qiana's lip turn up in a wicked smile…it was just for a second, but they could have sworn they saw it.

"Yeah, I had this friend once," Rashawn began and in minutes her comment drifted onto a tale of lurid passion and illicitness.

"To show you how much nothing it is…Rashawn, you can come. It's at my parent's," Qiana invited. Rashawn waved her hand.

"I'm too tired from moving this stuff. My back is hurtin'."

"My back is hurtin', my shoes too tight, my booty shaking from left to right…" Rita sang the childhood jingle, as she bumped hips with Qiana.

The women then giggled like schoolgirls.

Nigel arrived, right on time. He wore dark slacks, a dark turtleneck and jacket. Qiana stared for a moment before letting him in.

"You look great. I look…" She looked down at her ever-growing belly.

"You look beautiful," he smiled. He had been saying nice things to her on a regular basis now. It seemed to come easier for him lately.

Her hair, without the braids, had more than cleared her shoulders now and with the change in hormones, it was continuing to grow like crazy. She wore it down. He hadn't seen it this way before and ran his large hands down the length of it and then lightly caressed her face. "I like this," he added to the compliment. Before he knew it he had kissed her.

"I'm sorry," he said quickly.

"We said we wouldn't," she reminded him…and herself, of their commitment to keep this a platonic relationship between them.

"Then I'm really sorry," he said again.

She kissed him this time.

"I'm sorry we said that too," she giggled and began to lead him towards her bedroom. "Wanna see the house?" she said still giggling, as she began, what was yet to be another bogus tour…this surely was to be at least the third tour…of her house, anyway.

He began to remove his jacket.

"Nice bed where did you get it?" he asked…again.

"*Bed World,*" she giggled.

Nigel couldn't resist her smile. He had tried, but each day, each week that went by she became more and more endeared to him. Maybe it was her humble ways, her soft voice. Maybe it was the way she would curl her lip when he would say something stupid…he didn't know what it was, but he was falling for her and he couldn't stop.

He was surprised at how easy her belly was to maneuver around. It was getting very large and the baby was moving around constantly. But he was never surprised at how wonderful making love to her was. The way she would run her fingers though his hair and how her eyes would close right before he would kiss her…

He hadn't wanted to disappoint the guys, especially Smithy, but he, for a long time now, had the 'Black Chick' part of his dream figured out…if nothing else.

Over dinner, Andrew tried not to notice his daughter's constant blush every time this man, Nigel, would speak.

'*He seems bright enough…for a lawyer*', Andrew thought of Nigel. *Lawyers weren't his favorite people but he could live with it. It wasn't like Qiana was going to marry him. He had just donated sperm for her pregnancy. He was surprised at how easily they had all adjusted to this, but it was better then her having an affair with him.*

"So my mom lives in South San Francisco. She's a piano teacher," Nigel said. He was talking alot and in full animation, but he couldn't stop himself. He felt very good, complete, and happy.

"So, Godwins, is that a Jewish name?" Andrew asked, trying to identify what kind of ethnicity lied in Nigel's features.

"No, I'm Italian. Actually, only half, my father's name is Montgomery. His family is from England. He's a local judge here in the city. His father's first name was Nigel. But my grandmother gave me the last name of Godwins. It means God will win. It's kind of a long story." Nigel couldn't believe he had finally said it. For the first time since leaving Judge Montgomery's chambers, he had told someone the truth about who he really was.

"So what is involved in sperm donation?" Charles asked, out of the blue. Selena nudge him. "I was just kidding," he joked. Everyone laughed.

Only Chalice noticed her sister and this man...giving each other *that* look. It was only for a second but she had caught it. It was the look secret lovers give each other over a crowded room...or over her parent's table.

"I think your parents liked me," Nigel said with a light tone in his voice, as they drove home.

"That's good," Qiana said, looking out the window. "I don't expect to meet your mom. But that's ok," Qiana said finally after some quiet moments. Nigel hadn't thought about it.

He hadn't given much thought to where their newfound relationship was headed. He enjoyed Qiana's company and her friendship. It was true her tender affection had become something, he could no longer do without, but he hadn't given much thought beyond that. He hadn't thought about how she would fit into other parts of his life; he had been so wrapped up in only this part. He hadn't thought about visitation of the child, nor had the thought about his mother's involvement with little Ana...It wasn't like he and Qiana were married...

"It's ok," Qiana said, bringing Nigel's attention back to their conversation. He realized his mind had drifted and what she had said was more of a request, than a comment.

"Well..." he began slowly, trying to find the right answer to what he sensed should have been an easy question, but for some reason, it was not.

"That's ok."

"No, it's not ok. Its not you, it's me. I can't explain it but it's kinda personal," he said.

Personal...His life...Not hers; she heard that loud and clear.

Nigel sensed something was changing suddenly between them. Somewhere between her parent's house and *The Palemos* they had just broken up and he didn't even know they were officially 'together'.

"Can I come in?" he asked, as he pulled in front of the house.

"No, I'm tired," she smiled politely. "But thanks for going with me. I appreciate it; you didn't have to do that," she continued on cordially.

"Qiana, I wanted too; we're friends right?"

"Yeah, sure, friends. Thanks again." She smiled and climbed out of the car without even a kiss goodnight.

Business as usual...that was Qiana.

He watched her walk up to the door and then go inside.

He figured it out.... he would just never get it right with women...it was just that simple.

Qiana took off her light jacket and laid it across the unmade bed...their bed.

Nigel had helped her pick it out. She had made the decision to get rid of the bed she and Russell had shared during their relationship.

This bed was a large four-poster canopy bed, made out of beige twisted wood, draped with a sheer veil, for the canopy and dressed in dark rich colors. 'Now that's a bed made for fantasies,' Nigel had said. His eyes light up when they passed the display in the store...he had it delivered to her house the next day.

Her mind soared to the fresh memory of Nigel and her making love in that bed the first time...and again this time. He was always so tender, so loving...She couldn't believe a man so detached from everything and everyone around him could be so considerate in bed, making sure she was comfortable and feeling just right. Russell never made sure of anything except that he had another condom waiting...just in case.

She knew they were more than 'just friends'. Nigel had to realized that too...he was just being stubborn...

Just then there was a hard knock on the door. 'It had to be Nigel', she thought. He had come back to clear things up. He always came back. She knew he had to have thought about what he had said…He had to feel more for her then just friendship.

She wanted him.

It didn't matter if she never met his mother or anyone else in his life…

She wanted him.

It wasn't for the baby's sake anymore…

She wanted him.

She swung the door open only to find not Nigel…but Russell.

He looked different…high…dangerous. It was like he was half-Rufus and half-Russell now. What had happened to him in the last five months?

She didn't want to find out.

"Russell how did you find me?" she asked, showing instant alarm.

"Nosy neighbors. They seen ya people and ya white man movin' you out my lady," he answered. "They heard you say *The Palemos*…So I'm tinkin…Paleeemos…my lady, she be movin' on up like the *Jeffersons*. Then I thought, Jefferson…funny, he had a black mistress too, and then I got mad all ova again," he said and then pushed his way into her home.

"Russell you need to leave," she ordered.

"Leave? But you got so much room here," he said looking around, noticing the baby things that Nigel had helped her pick out. He then noticed the beautifully dressed cradle and pushed it over with his foot. Qiana ran to set it back up. Russell grabbed her and slapped her hard.

"But does he luv you right my lady? Can he give it to you like your Rufus?" he breathed heavily in her face. His breath reeked and she could tell he hadn't bathed recently.

She tried to scream but couldn't. As he ran his hands over her belly, she pulled away and ran for the door only to be tackled to the floor. She scrambled to her feet and reached the door. Out of the corner of her eye she could have swore she saw the shimmering edge of the blade.

Nigel hadn't been able to go to sleep. He wanted to talk to Qiana. He wanted to clear everything up. He didn't know what that meant, but it sounded good when he said it out loud. He didn't know what he needed to say, but he needed to say something.

The phone rang.

"Nigel you've got to come to the hospital, it's Qiana!" Rashawn cried into the phone.

By the look on Terrell's face when he burst into the emergency room he knew it wasn't good.

"Where is Qiana?" Nigel charged Terrell, who stood with his hands deep in his pockets. Nigel had never seen him look so meek before. Terrell licked his lips and composed himself before his spoke.

"Qiana is fine," he began. Nigel sensed the words to follow but he had to ask.

"And Ana?" he asked of the baby.

Rita, upon hearing the affection in Nigel's voice, as he addressed the baby by the name he and Qiana had agreed she would be named, began to cry and quickly walked out of the emergency room.

Terrell shook his head.

"Qiana's ex beat her up Nigel. I don't know how to soften it, man. He beat her pretty bad," Terrell sighed heavily before continuing. "Now, she lost a lot of blood, but she got here in time."

As Terrell spoke the room around them seem to blur.

"He cut her..." Terrell used his hands against his own body to show Nigel the six inches or more across her stomach that Russell's knife had gone in, ripping the life from Ana. "And when the police came he resisted arrest and he was shot and killed."

"What?" Nigel asked, as he had missed the last thing Terrell said.

Terrell put his arm around Nigel's shoulder as he spoke.

"The police came?" Nigel asked, as if trying to stay a part of the conversation, although, his mind was drifting. "And he's dead now," Nigel's words sounded distant from the situation.

Terrell's mouth dried, as he spoke.

"The neighbors called the cops when they saw Qiana run out of the house and that guy following her with the knife...and you know *The Palemos*, there's a cop on every corner," Terrell chuckled in a nervous mannerism, noticing the color leaving Nigel's face. "He didn't actually cut her until they were outside, so it wasn't like the cops weren't sure of what was going on," Terrell continued to relate the information given him from the police. Nigel was nodding as Terrell spoke, though Terrell could tell he was only half listening.

"Now what did you say again?" Nigel asked. His mind was in a fog now, as his thoughts had drifted back to her beautiful face, her soft small hands...to the movement inside her belly...the way her eyes would close...

"Where is my baby?" Daphne exclaimed as she exploded into the emergency room in full hysteria. Andrew wasn't far behind in distance, or emotion.

When Rashawn appeared from the elevator. She saw Nigel and her heart sank. He had come just like she knew he would.

How could she tell him that Qiana didn't want to see him? That she didn't ever want to see him again. She had only been conscious for a few moments and that was all she had said.

"Nigel I'm so glad you came," Daphne said as she held his hands tight. "I knew you cared. I could tell you really cared," she said.

"The baby is gone. It was a girl you know," was all he could say, as he felt his link with these wonderful people about to fade into a mere acquaintance.

The doctor appeared and looked around for a relative. Daphne and Andrew stepped forward and together with the doctor; they walked a little ways from the others to learn of the condition of their daughter.

"We've moved her upstairs. She's stable now and it looks like we have most of situation under control. If it's any help, any help at all, the sacrifice of the child was a lifesaver to your daughter. If she hadn't been pregnant she would have died," Nigel heard the doctor say to her parents.

"Is she going to be able to get pregnant again? Can she have another baby?" Daphne's voice trembled with the question. Nigel found himself straining to hear the answer.

"Thank God," he heard Andrew sigh.

"It's gonna be all right Nyge. Qiana is a tough chick under that soft front she puts on," Terrell smiled broadly in his attempts to console his friend. Nigel just nodded and watched the Pattersons' talking with the doctor.

He wanted to walk over there. He wanted to be told directly what was going on. He didn't want to be on the fringes of Qiana's life this way. But he knew he had no place here…not really. He was just the sperm donor.

By morning Nigel had to accept that Qiana wasn't going to see him. She had been awake off and on through the night but still she refused to see him.

He walked out of the hospital. The sun was bright and it hurt his eyes. He had left his sunglasses at home in his hurry to get there the night before.

Terrell and the others had left many hours ago; only Daphne remained behind. She was the one who had to finally break it to him that Qiana did not want to see him.

"She just told me to tell you 'thank you for everything'. She…" Daphne hugged him. "She's just very hurt, Nigel."

"Yeah, me too," he said and forced a smile.

"Why won't she see me? What did I do that was so wrong?" Nigel asked his grandfather as they again strolled together in the park near his mother's house.

It had been a week and finally he felt he could talk about it. His grandfather had been a good listening ear.

"Nothing. You tried," he said.

"I feel awful. I feel like if she hadn't been pregnant, none of this would have happened. I feel like it's all my fault."

"Why?"

"Because I got her pregnant," Nigel blurted out.

"You didn't get her pregnant. She got herself pregnant. But then maybe that's why she won't see you, I mean…it was only business, right? And now the business is over," he said.

"I just can't get over it like that," Nigel admitted.

"Why?" his grandfather asked again.

"Because I think…" Nigel choked back the words.

"You think? That's wonderful. You're a lawyer who thinks," his grandfather joked sarcastically.

"I think I love her," Nigel said and then took a deep breath.

"Now was that so hard?" his grandfather smiled. "You love her," he said and his smile grew even wider. Nigel didn't know why his grandfather was grinning so wide.

Couldn't his grandfather tell he was dying inside?

CHAPTER 14

It had been almost four months since Qiana had lost the baby. If anyone were looking on, it would have appeared to him or her standing there on the outside, that everything had gone back to normal in Nigel's life.

He had gone back to winning cases while still avoiding Judge Montgomery's courtroom and he and Terrell still played golf or tennis most Sunday's with Smithy and all his offbeat yet quite profound wisdom. Smithy was planning to take the bar soon and now his thoughts were deeper than ever.

Anyone looking on from the outside would surely feel that this year had been erased from everyone's life.

The only exception to normalcy was that Rita and Terrell had married in a quiet civil ceremony. She was six months pregnant with twins and now, feeling awkward every time she saw Nigel or Qiana.

Terrell saw Nigel everyday and though Nigel would smile and act the same, he had to admit that his friend had changed somehow, although, neither of them was about to say a word about it.

He knew Nigel went home every night to that empty condo and no doubt rarely slept. His usual crisp and tightly wrapped exterior had somehow changed, to one worn by a man who had been through it...and lost. He had stopped taking on domestic cases and was now doing more corporate work. Cases that had no faces attached...just numbers and dollar signs.

Nigel's smile, lack the same luster and he just didn't seem happy anymore. Rita had plagued Terrell to tell Nigel that Qiana too had been miserable, though she too had gone on with her life like nothing had happened. She had gone on like her life could just go back to the way it was before the baby...before she had fallen so deeply in love with Nigel.

"I can't say that," Terrell would tell her.

"You mean you won't. What, is it a silly guy's thing? I've seen Nigel when he comes over. He's so unhappy. He loves her and you can tell he misses her. I think he hopes to run into her over here or something. I mean I've seen him drive clear out of the way to avoid that corner up there," Rita said, pointing in the direction of Qiana's house. "And they both act like they don't see me all big and pregnant. I'm getting tired of trying to hide it. Let alone...unable."

"Qiana is in love with him. She can't even say his name without crying. You know she hasn't even returned all the baby stuff they bought. It's all in that spare room, it's just in there. I worry about her," Rashawn chimed in.

"This is something they have to work out. It's going to take time and it's none of our business," Terrell defended.

The girls would cut their eyes at him and Rita would simply waddle into the kitchen and treat him coldly for a while before moving on to something else to fuss about.

Marriage to Rita had filled Terrell more than he wanted to admit. His decision to live there with her and her sister instead of moving Rita away from that neighborhood had turned out to be the best decision he had ever made. Living there, next door to their aunt and across the street from their cousin and with the twins coming gave him a sense of family, of belonging to someone other than himself. He felt bad for Nigel not having that...after coming so close.

He feared Nigel might do something drastic soon.

It had been the hardest search he had ever made for anything but he had found it. There, in that old record store on Main Street in Santa Cruz, he had located it. It was in the used record department. The cover was kind of beat up but the clerk promised that the record was not scratched in the least.

"You can return it if I'm wrong, no prob," the longhaired hippie wannabe smiled, as he put it in the bag and handed the LP to Nigel.

"Oh, even if it's scratched I won't be returning it," Nigel smiled to himself, knowing that just having the record was going to take care of most of the problem. It wasn't like he had a ready turntable to hear it right away.

Finding one of those was going to be another adventure in itself.

When Qiana heard the knock on the door, she peeked out the window only to see the brown BMW parked across the street under the large tree that dropped the big leaves and made a mess of the street, when the winds would come through and beat it all up.

"Qiana," she heard him call through the door. Once again she felt the softness in his voice and it affected her, just like the first time she heard it in the clinic on that cassette. She stood for a long time behind the door, until he called again.

"Nigel, please go away," she called softly.

Those were the first words he had heard from her in months.

"No, actually I won't. I want to see you. I need to talk to you. We have some unfinished business."

She hadn't been back to work since leaving the hospital and even now, though her disability had run out, she just couldn't face that office with all those children. She hadn't paid her rent to Nigel in months either, and her savings account was nearly empty.

"And what would that be," she said, swinging the door open. He was wearing that hunter green shirt she liked so much, khaki pants, and boat shoes without socks. The shirt gave his hazel eyes that greener direction, which she found hard to look into directly, without her heart starting to race. The wind was up and had blown his hair wildly.

"The money? Are you here to get the money I owe?" Qiana said coldly.

Nigel stepped in. He looked around her living room. She had finished decorating it completely and it was as he had imagined, complete with crocheted dollies, which she had made.

"What Nigel?" she asked curtly, bringing him back to the now. He looked at her. Her eyes were moist, as if possibly she had cried just recently. Though she had lost a lot of weight, her face was still round...*that cute round face that always made him smile.*

"Hold on," he said abruptly bounding out the door to his car. She watched as he opened the trunk and unloaded what seemed to be a small stereo system. She stood out of his way while he made three trips out to his car until he had brought the whole thing in, complete with both speakers. He sat it up under the window on a small table and placed a record on the turntable to play. It was a scratchy yet non-skipping old *Born Steady* album. One of their older ones...the one that had all those slow sensuous songs...

He laid the needle so carefully about half way through the one side and caught the beginning of the song just right.

Before she could stop him, he had taken her in his arms and together they began to sway to the tune that had played in his mind constantly for months, and now poured out that stereo...*For Love's Sake.* Now he knew the name to match the tune, now he knew the feelings to match the name.

It had taken twelve records stores before anyone had it in stock, but now he had it, the song from the dream.

And now he would make the moment...well sort of...there was no yacht. Smithy never did get that part figured out.

Perhaps if Qiana wanted, they could take a cruise for their honeymoon...

"Nigel, what is going on?" he heard her whisper.

"Whatever it is, it has to be for love's sake this time," he said and then he kissed her, a deep kiss, which she returned.

Epilogue

He neared the lookout of the Golden Gate Bridge. The fog had just begun to settle in and the boats passing under the bridge gave out their warning. One was a large yacht…a party boat, with ribbons and dancing people. He couldn't resist the urge to wave at them, as this was a very happy day for him. It was his wedding day and he had appointment with an angel. As he turned, she approached. She was dressed in a flowing white dress and her hair framed her round face. She was beautiful, glowing, as she walked towards him. He looked around towards the crowd gathered there at the lookout. They were all smiling and pointing at the boat. "We'll be meeting them soon," someone said…Nigel knew he had heard it this time; he heard it clearly. The woman called his name and he turned his attention back to her. He took her small hand in his and together they walked towards crowd of waiting people. The crowd began to cheer and wave. As the wind picked up, her dress blew, clinging to her body. He looked for the signs of her pregnancy but there was only a small bulge that he was sure only he noticed. Music filled the air now…That old familiar tune, but today he knew both the name and who wrote it. He looked deep into his beauty's eyes and then kissed her. "For love's sake," she whispered in his ear…and he heard her this time…Because, this time…it wasn't a dream.

THE END

ABOUT THE AUTHOR

A native Californian, the Author, Michelle McGriff has been writing full-time while completing her BA in English. Enjoying this avenue of alternative publishing, Ms. McGriff has been able to get her stories to the audience they deserve…you. With stories like *Majestic Secret* and *For Love's Sake*, and even more short stories in the works, she hopes that you enjoy them all as much as she enjoyed writing them.